SPIRITBOUND

SPELLBOUND SERIES

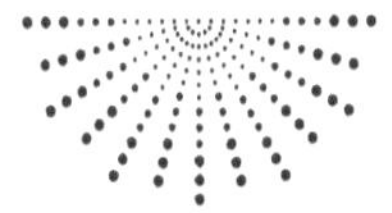

DANI KRISTOFF

Spiritbound was first published by Harlequin Enterprises in 2015.
This version is published by Australian Speculative Fiction in 2019

ISBN 978-1-922360-51-9 (ebook)

ISBN Print 978-1-922360-01-04

Cover by Bookcover4u.com

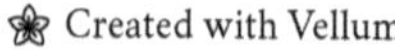 Created with Vellum

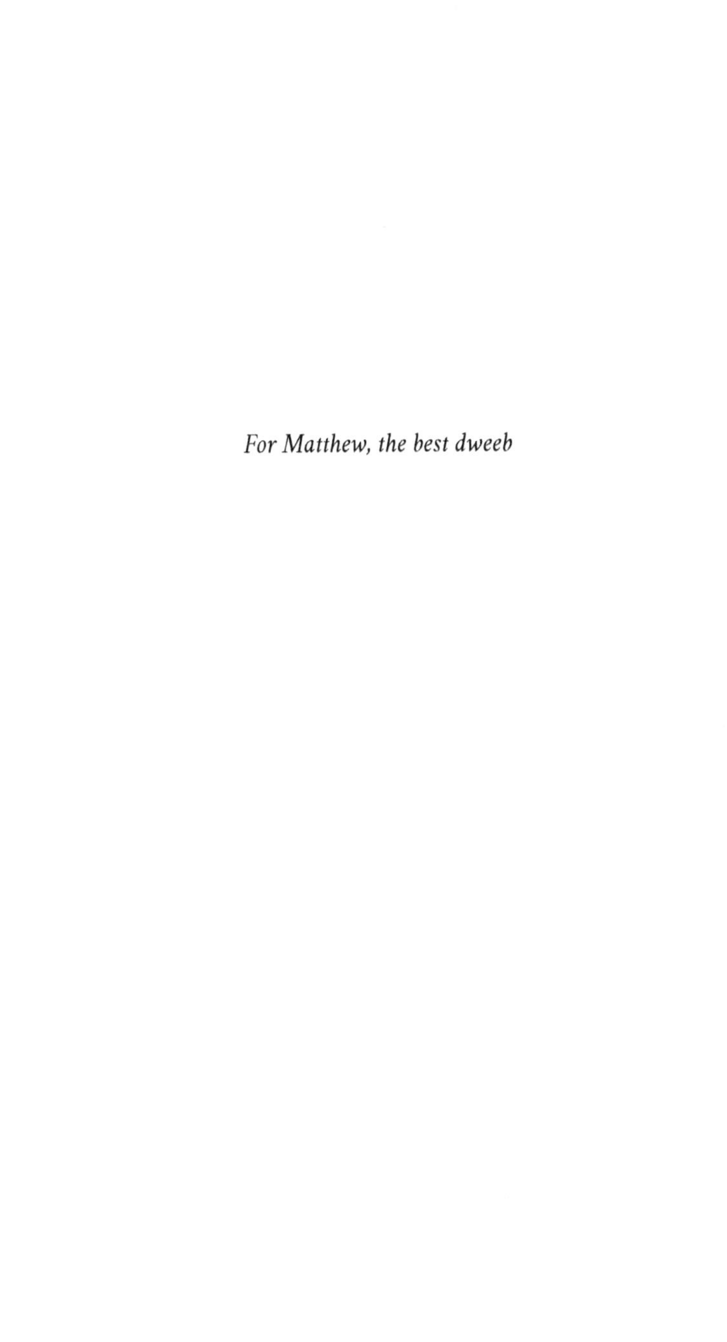

For Matthew, the best dweeb

PROLOGUE

In the back garden, Grace Riordon knelt on the grass and patted down the soil around the dandelion she had planted. The little willow tree cast shade over her as she picked up the trowel and pushed it into the ground to make another hole. A presence brushed her mind. With a smile, she turned. It was Declan. 'Are you going to take all day with that?' he asked, a twinkle in his dark eyes.

No, she thought at him. She smiled when their minds touched briefly. Declan fell back a step.

Amazing, he thought back at her. Your essence is so strong; so full of life.

The week before, they'd accidentally touched minds. Declan had said it was her talent, rather than his. Actually he'd likened her ability to reach out to him as an unpredictable jack-in-the-box. She smiled, remembering her first encounter with his golden essence. At first she didn't know what she'd done, until he'd turned to her and sent her a thought so vivid and strong that she'd nearly passed out. After that she'd wanted more.

Apparently witches her age weren't meant to be able to do such things. Deciding between them that they best keep quiet about it, they carried on as normal and limited touching minds. Parents were strange about things like that and they'd fret and worry that such closeness, such a bond at an early age, would be detrimental to both of them. Only yesterday she had heard her mother talking to Matilda, saying she was concerned about how much time she spent with Declan.

'Can I help?' he asked, squatting down beside her.

She shoved the trowel into the dirt to make another hole. 'Mother wants me to plant these in a particular way. It won't take long. Why don't you see what Elena's doing?'

Declan smiled at her. Grace beamed back, unable to hide her love. He messed her hair. 'Okay, but don't take long or we'll come to get you.'

He touched his mind to hers and she gasped. She saw the love he had for her. She sighed, knowing that one day they'd be together and never part.

He sauntered around to the front of the house to find her cousin, Elena. Being closer in age, they had a good friendship and could keep each other amused while Grace finished her chores. With a sigh, Grace picked up one of the plants and placed it gently into the soil and covered it up, repeating the incantation her mother had drilled into her that morning. Then, scooting over a bit on her knees, she dug the trowel in again and repeated the process. She rubbed her nose on her forearm, accidentally dropping soil into her hair. She shook her head vigorously and then reached for the next plant.

A piercing scream made her skin tingle and her breath catch. Immediately dropping the trowel, Grace jumped up, knowing in her gut that something awful had happened to Elena. The tremor in her heartbeat and the butterflies running rampant in her stomach were a dead giveaway. She and Elena had always had a connection, unable to shield each other against each other's distress. Bolting around the side of the house, she couldn't see Elena in the front garden. Two tennis rackets lay on the thick, green grass, a threadbare ball close by. Where had she and Declan gotten to?

Another cry from Elena and Grace turned, catching sight of her cousin as she knelt on the side of the road, huddled over. Declan squatted behind her, rubbing her back. His soothing tones reached Grace. She rushed over, the scene opening up as she approached. Fel, the cat, lay on the tarmac, blood leaking from its head.

Elena screamed again, dissolving into tears.

Grace dashed over. 'Oh no,' she said as she bent down to examine the treasured pet. 'What happened?'

Her questioning gaze met Declan's. 'A car ran over it,' he replied, then chewed on his bottom lip.

Elena's green irises were vivid against the bloodshot whites. Such distress twisted Grace's insides.

Grace reached out with her talent, touched Declan's mind gently and was overwhelmed by the turmoil inside of him. He blamed himself for the cat being injured and hearing Elena scream had been torment. She moved her talent away, realising that he was so distracted, he hadn't even noticed her touch. 'It's dead,' he added, his voice gravelly.

Grace glanced at the cat and rolled her eyes. 'Don't be silly,' she said, as Elena began wailing again, placing the cat on her lap.

'Elena, let me see.' Elena nodded, her fists rubbing against her swollen red eyes. Grace gently took Fel from Elena's hold.

Her cousin then chewed her knuckles as tears

continued to roll unabated down her cheeks while she watched Grace examine the cat.

Grace sent her talent into the small furry body. She could sense it there, its life—just hovering on the brink. She couldn't let Elena lose her pet; couldn't see her suffer. 'It's not dead. See.' She gave a little tug and life surged back into the cat.

Declan reeled and fell back on his hands. 'What did you do?' His dark eyes bored into hers. His sweet face was marred by horror, his eyes wide and mouth agape.

'Nothing. I just called to the cat.'

They all looked down. The cat's translucent body rose up, leaving the bloody, furry mass behind. Elena sucked in a surprised breath. 'Fel?' The cat meowed, but it sounded unearthly.

The hairs on the back of Grace's neck stood erect. One look at Elena revealed that her mouth was open but nothing came out.

Fel's ghost rubbed itself against Elena's knee.

Instinctively, she reached for Declan with her talent and cried out at what she found in his mind. Horror engulfed him; revulsion and fear tinged his golden essence with fingers of brown. It was then she knew she'd done wrong. Declan met her gaze and shook his head. Then like shutters slamming down, he blocked her from reaching him.

She jerked back and blinked at the suddenness of it. 'Declan?'

The front door slammed. Her mother was coming. Declan backed away from her, shaking his head.

'What is it?' she asked. 'What have I done? Please.'

'You're a necromancer!' Declan's face was pale.

The way he looked at her cut her to the core. 'A what?'

'You raise the dead.'

Grace frowned. 'Don't be silly. It wasn't dead.'

'Yes, it was. Look at it. You've animated its undead spirit. Only evil, dark witches raise the dead.' All trace of Declan's softness was gone. He was angry, afraid.

Grace sucked in a breath. Oh goddess, he was afraid of her. She tried to touch his mind again, but was met with a hard wall.

Please Declan, she thought at him. Don't shut me out. Don't hide from me.

But he wouldn't answer.

Grace didn't want to look at Fel. The force of Declan's rejection shocked her. Yet the cat's body sat there and its ghostly form was kneading its paws on Elena's knee. Elena's wide, green eyes stared at the cat, then lifted to Grace, her face clouded in puzzlement.

Fel lifted its head and let out a melancholy cry. Declan jumped back as if stung. His eyes were large, his mouth ajar. He shook his head. 'No, this is wrong. It can't be.'

His attention shifted to Grace. There was hatred in his eyes and his fists were clenched. Grace's world crashed around her as his negative emotions washed over her. 'You broke the law, Grace. You'll be punished, cast out of the coven.'

'I didn't mean it. Please, Declan, don't say that.'

'It's true. There's no stopping it.'

Her eyes burned with tears. 'But you're my friend, Declan. Nothing can change that.'

Standing over her, he shook his head. His body was stiff with outrage. 'I can never see you again, Grace. You've gone too far.' He turned and bolted down the street. Grace watched his retreating back, tears streaming down her cheeks.

Her mother, Elvira, appeared, hands on hips, her

gaze fixed on the retreating back of Declan Mallory. 'Well, now. I never thought to see that Mallory spooked by one of the Denholm clan. I thought he was made of stronger stuff.' Grace sat very still. What had she done? She'd broken the law. Her heart was beating double time. Elena reached over and squeezed her hand.

Grace began to babble. 'I didn't mean to do anything wrong, Mother. I thought...I thought it was still alive. It was there. I mean, I could feel Fel. Just there, and I called to her. Like I—'

'There now, don't fret.' Elvira patted Grace on the head and then bent to survey the cat. When she put out a hand, Fel rubbed her head against it. 'It's Fel alright. The cat always was a bit unusual. Descended from a long line of folk-bred felines, so it's not surprising it wasn't going to die like a normal one. A strong spirit, and attached to Elena, is my guess. No wonder it was just there waiting for you to fetch it back.'

She stood up straight. 'Come along then. We best bury the body in the garden and then prepare for a council meeting. They'll be here soon, I suspect.'

'Will they send me away?' Grace asked as she cradled Fel's cooling body. 'Declan said I'd be cast out.'

'No, my darling girl, of course not. You're just thirteen years old. The statute doesn't cover minors. But they're sure going to make a song and dance about it. I doubt this will be forgotten for a long time. You may suffer for it in other ways.'

'Declan said he could never see me again.' Grace wiped at the moisture on her face.

Elvira tilted her head to the side as she considered this. 'He may not be able to, my darling. Right now he's scared but he'll get over it. Unfortunately, I can't see his mother allowing him to associate with you again. Not after this.'

'But we—'

'I know, my darling girl, but there are some folk that you can't reason with and Delores Mallory is queen among them. Don't worry about it for now. You're too young to form a lasting passion. You'll see. Declan Mallory will be a distant memory when you're older.'

Elvira squatted down and scooped up their pet's body.

A punch to the stomach couldn't have wounded Grace more. Forget Declan, after what they'd shared? Not possible. Grace buried her face into her mother's side and sobbed into her skirt. Elena hiccuped and took Elvira's other hand as they headed around the back. The ghostly cat followed along behind them, its tail down, as if it knew the gravity of the situation.

❀

Grace and Elena sat in the dark hallway, peering into the lounge room and listening to the council proceedings.

'You're saying Grace didn't know what she was about? Didn't know she was performing a forbidden act?' This was Mr Mallory, Declan's father.

'Yes, that's exactly what I'm saying. Grace is not scheduled to be taught about the forbidden arts until next year, and how not to perform them until the year after that.'

'My son said she did it without effort, without thinking.'

Elvira nodded. 'Yes, she did.' Grace heard the pride in her mother's voice and didn't understand it.

'A powerful witch then. Such skill and strength in

one so young,' commented Martha Burton, one of the elder witches. 'Do you think she can be cured of her tendency for necromancy?'

A few of the gathered witches and warlocks twitched and made signs of protection.

Her mother stood up and straightened her shoulders. 'Martha, I think my daughter would have to do more than bring a cat back to life by accident to be considered to have a tendency, don't you think? You have not considered the nature of the cat. This is no stray tabby we are talking about, but a cat descended from a long line of folk-bred felines.'

'She should be ostracized,' Mr Mallory said, pointing a finger at Elvira. 'Sent up north. Away from here. She's a dark witch. She belongs there.'

Elvira sucked in a huge breath. 'My daughter is not a dark witch.'

Martha drew herself up to her full height. 'Enough!' Elvira and Declan's father blinked and then faced the elder. 'Mallory,' Martha continued, 'I have examined the child and she is not touched by dark. We will not be sending one of our most talented witches away to be taught by other less-than-savoury elements in a breakaway coven in the north. She will remain here.'

'But—' he began to argue.

'She will be punished.'

'How?' Elvira asked, her voice carrying a hard edge.

Elena squeezed Grace's hand. Grace lowered her eyes and bit her lip. This was awful.

'For one year, Grace is to be taught at home. She is not to socialise with other members of the coven. Tutors will be assigned to her, and she will be drilled in the forbidden arts, starting tomorrow. At the end of the year, she will be tested.'

'And if she doesn't pass your test?'

'Then, Elvira, you will have a choice to relocate with your daughter.'

Mr Mallory shook his head. 'You're too lenient. I won't have the girl near my son anymore. He's spent too much time with her already. You've all been concerned, given their ages.'

'It's true; the coven has been concerned. But we have trusted in Declan to treat her with care.'

Mr Mallory scoffed. 'What about keeping him safe from her? She's a bad influence.'

Elvira scoffed. 'He's a young, fifteen-year-old boy. A good boy. A warlock of no mean talent. How could my thirteen-year-old daughter harm him? You're being ridiculous.'

'Now, Elvira, let's not inflame the situation,' Martha interjected.

Mr Mallory paced the room. 'I won't put up with this insolence from her. We're leaving Sydney and that's it.'

'A sad loss to us, Mallory,' Martha Burton said. 'Are you sure such delicacy is necessary? I understood the young people had formed an attachment—'

'Absolutely not,' he sneered at Elvira. 'Not with a member of the Denholm clan. We let them play together, to mingle, but no more.'

The heavy push of tears made Grace lower her head.

'There is a very good school in England. My mother has connections there. We shall make arrangements to leave immediately.' He turned to the other members of the council and bowed to them. 'I will take my leave of you."

As the door slammed after him, Elvira sighed. 'A bit of an overreaction, don't you think?'

'For Mallory? I don't think so,' commented

Martha. 'He's been highly strung for years. You forget what happened. Then there's that wife of his. There's no need to remind you of the bad blood there.'

Elvira met her stare. 'No, I don't forget anything.'

'Elvira will you accept the judgement on behalf of your daughter?'

'I will.' Her words were ground out.

'Then we will leave you.'

Elena tugged on Grace's arm, pulling her back into their shared bedroom. As she lay in the dark, silent tears bathing her face, she knew it could have been worse. Yet she'd lost her best friend, forever. Her heart was irretrievably broken. She wasn't allowed to talk to her other friends for a year. It was too much to bear.

Elena wrapped her arms around her. At least they had each other. The image of Declan and the look of revulsion on his face stayed with her. She'd thought they'd had shared a special bond. They had touched each other's minds. But that was all to be forgotten now.

CHAPTER ONE

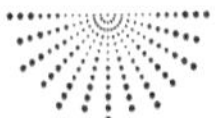

Grace entered through the front door of the community hall and searched the crowd for Elena. Her cousin chatted gaily with Danila Newman, a witch from Cronulla. Elena must have made a joke because Danila threw back her head to laugh, sending her sun-bleached hair rippling down her back. Grace stood a little taller and headed over.

'Grace, you made it.' Elena swooped in with a kiss to her cheek, then gestured with her glass. 'You know Danila Newman, don't you?'

Grace hadn't spoken to Danila for more than nine years. Grace put out her hand. 'Hi, I've not seen you in an age.' Danila's gaiety fled and her dark blue eyes dropped to Grace's proffered hand. The young witch lifted her chin, made a scoffing noise and turned away.

'Ouch,' Grace said with a cheerful grin as she watched Danila disappear into the crowd.

Elena swung around, gaping at the departing witch. 'The nerve of her. I thought all that stopped years ago.'

'Mostly. Gee, it's packed in here.' Grace put on a big smile and snaffled a glass of sparkling wine from a passing tray. She took a sip, her gaze traveling over the crowd, searching for anyone she knew or who cared to acknowledge her.

Elena rubbed her back. 'I can't believe some people still hold grudges. The council lifted the sanctions on you when you were fourteen and you've been a model witch since then. Is this why we didn't have a party last year for your twenty-first?'

Grace shrugged. 'Maybe.' Her mother had thought it best to have a quiet celebration, although reaching twenty-one was considered a major milestone for one of the folk. Most families celebrated with the whole coven. Taking a mate was equally important and also celebrated, something Grace hadn't done either. No warlock came near her.

Being a couple of years older when she came to live with them, Elena hadn't gone to their special school. Elvira hadn't thought it was necessary because Elena was a half-witch. So her adopted sister hadn't seen first-hand the slights Grace had endured. Then again without the distraction of having friends, Grace had excelled in her studies. Unfortunately, that only made matters worse. The more she excelled, the more she was hated. Then she'd become such a good witch, people were afraid of her. The label necromancer was firmly stuck to her hide.

A tray full of yummy hors d'Oeuvres passed by and Grace grabbed a few before the waiter disappeared into the crowd. 'Want one?' she asked, with her mouth half full as she offered a prawn and avocado titbit to Elena.

'No. I already ate a heap before you got here. The smoked salmon and mayo ones are divine by the way.'

'So what's new?' Grace asked as Elena eyed the crowd. 'Anyone interesting?' Someone interesting was usually someone from another coven who they didn't know and who would talk to them, because they didn't know about Grace's reputation.

Elena started. 'No. No.' She shook her head, and threads of red hair floated free from her chignon. 'No one you'd be interested in.'

Grace's scalp crawled with her third sense. 'What is it? There's something you're not telling me. Spit it out.'

Elena shrugged. 'Oh, just a rumor.'

Grace looked around, her sense of unease growing. 'What rumor?'

Elena sighed, then leaned in to speak into her ear. 'The Mallorys are here tonight.'

Grace's heart skipped a beat. 'Oh, great.'

Elena frowned and looked at her feet. 'Yes, I'm sorry.'

'He's here, isn't he?'

Elena's head shot up. 'Don't do this to yourself.'

'Too late. I'm determined to rid myself of his ghost.' Grace darted off into the crowd, determined to find a good vantage point from which to view her first love. Was he as scrawny and gangly as she remembered? Was he still holier-than-thou? Would he still be afraid of her? That brought a smile to her face.

Her emotions span out of control as well. There was anxiety and excitement fluttering in her stomach. She didn't think she'd react this way. It was not a good sign. After all this time, she ought to be indifferent. She'd been so young when she had loved him, yet thoughts of him lingered. The hurt was just as raw as it had been that day. She'd not seen him for nearly nine years—a veritable lifetime. Would she even recognize him?

A tall warlock moved and there, in her line of sight, was Declan. It hit her like a physical punch. She wanted to slide back into the crowd so he wouldn't see her but she couldn't take her eyes off him. It was the Declan she knew, but not. He was a man now. He'd be twenty-four. He was tall, with dark hair and eyes that sat elegantly in high cheekbones. He smiled, and the sun rose inside her. Memories of that horrible day sped into her mind, but she flicked them off like flies. This was the moment she longed for and dreaded. He was talking to someone with long, blonde hair. The woman turned and she realized it was Danila and her heart sank. A gorgeous, blonde witch. Great. Declan threw back his head and laughed at something Danila said and then he looked directly at Grace, speared her with his gaze.

Blood thumped in Grace's ears. The voices around her merged into a thrum. There was only her and Declan. He smiled at her, white teeth dazzling in his shapely mouth. She returned the smile, yet she was wary. Maybe he didn't recognize her.

Next, he was excusing himself and heading in her direction. Panic stations blared in Grace's brain. *Oh goddess! What will I say?*

'Hello, I'm Declan Mallory.' He had a delicious British accent.

Her heart sunk. 'I know.'

He chuckled. 'I didn't think anyone would remember me. I've been gone so long.'

'Eight years, four months, five days.'

He frowned. 'What?'

Grace threw up a smile, even though she knew she was doomed. 'That's how long you've been gone.'

She exhaled slowly, waiting, just waiting for the penny to drop. He studied her face, her hair. 'Grace?'

Lowering her head, she stared at the floor, unable to meet his gaze, unwilling to see the hate.

A finger touched her chin, gently urged her face

up. 'You look stunning, Grace. I don't think I would've recognized you. You've changed so much.'

Her heart fluttered at the look of admiration on his face. 'You look pretty good yourself.' He'd removed his finger from her chin, but her skin still burned from his touch.

He chuckled then, but she could tell he was thinking about that day. It was a cloud shadowing his eyes.

Rose Mason, a tall, dark-haired witch came up. Grace suppressed a groan. Rose was arch enemy number one, being her chief tormenter in school. Grace kept her face devoid of emotion. 'Hi, Declan,' Rose said gaily. Tossing her dark curls over her shoulder, she smiled lusciously into his face. 'It's so good to meet you.' She edged between them, nudging Grace out. 'A group of us are getting together at Bondi Beach tomorrow. Please say you'll come.'

Declan frowned. 'Excuse me. I was talking to Grace. You do know Grace, don't you?' He stepped around Rose and nestled closer to Grace.

Rose turned slightly and lifted her nose. She smiled at Declan as if he'd not mentioned Grace at all. 'I can pick you up in the morning, if you like. Please say you'll come.'

'I'm sorry. I'm otherwise engaged. Won't you acknowledge Grace?'

Rose turned around. 'Riordon,' she said in a sulky voice.

'Hello, Rose,' Grace replied, shifting from foot to foot.

Declan's dark brows drew together as he narrowed his eyes at Rose. 'How can you be so rude?'

Of course it hurt being snubbed, but Grace had built up a tolerance for it. Still, having Declan notice and calling attention to it filled her with shame. It was as if the whole room was pointing at her, vilifying her, instead of just tolerating her. Forcing Rose to acknowledge her presence made Grace confront the ostracizm head-on, something she had not done for years. She held her breath, waiting for the inevitable backlash.

Rose backed up, taken aback by Declan's vehemence. 'She's a necromancer. Dark witch material.'

Grace's face heated. Why did she do that? Why remind Declan of that day?

Declan snorted then slid his hand to Grace's elbow and moved her away, without even saying goodbye to Rose. Grace took a deep breath to steady herself, using her talent to rid her face of the embarrassing blush.

He directed his gaze towards her and she flashed a weak smile.

'That makes me so angry,' he said to her. 'Please tell me that was a once-off.'

'I...um...' Her cheeks flamed again, her ability to use her talent momentarily gone. She couldn't tell him the truth. Nor could she come up with a fib, not with him touching her.

'Declan?'

It was his father. Grace's eyes met the old man's. Nothing had changed in the preceding years. They were still full of distrust and fear.

Declan waved. 'In a minute.' He turned back to her, a smile in his eyes. 'I thought about you a lot over the years. It's good to see you again.'

Grace smiled, detecting sincerity in his words. She dared not touch his mind or even mind speak him. 'I...er...'

'Declan?' His father called again more urgently, this time waving him over with vigorous movements.

Declan couldn't avoid seeing him. He sighed

loudly. 'Excuse me. I must go. I'll see you around.' Declan inclined his head, smiled briefly and left her.

Grace wanted to sink into the crowd, to slink away, but for some reason she stood there like a fool in full view. It wasn't hard to hear what Mr Mallory was saying. 'What are you doing talking to that woman?'

She had to use her talent to hear Declan's reply. 'I didn't recognize her, at first.'

'You know your mother will have one of her turns if she hears you were flirting with her.'

'Dad, I wasn't flirting. I was saying hello.'

'I forbid you to have anything to do with her, with any of that family.'

Declan nodded. 'Dad? Dad, you know I'm a man now. I make my own decisions.'

'Sure you do. I only meant it for the best.'

Declan cast a look over his shoulder and their eyes met. Grace turned her head away at the expression of regret she saw in them, then, unable to stop looking at him, unable to pass up the opportunity of fixing his image in her mind, she looked back.

His father put his arm over Declan's shoulder, urging him away. 'Don't go against me on this. Your mother's health wouldn't bear it. You know how she feels.'

Declan sighed and allowed himself to be introduced to a very eligible and attractive young witch called, Mira.

A depression began to fill Grace up as she surveyed the coven crowd. There were ten witches for every warlock in the room. Declan had a vast array of choices for a mate. It all became too much. Her feet leapt to obey her command and she fled the room. Elena hurried after her. 'Wait, Grace. Wait!'

Once outside, Grace sucked in the humid air. A summer Sydney night. A gentle harbor breeze.

'You okay?'

Grace gathered her arms over her chest and hugged herself. 'Yes.'

'You saw him then?'

'Yes,' Grace answered in an emotion-laden voice. 'Spoke to him too.'

'That's great.'

'Is it? He only talked to me because he didn't recognize me.' Her voice caught. She'd thought their reunion would be something more than a brief encounter. A bit more meaningful and deliberate than mistaken identity.

Elena put her arms around her. 'I know how you feel, Grace. I always have.'

'You do? Well, that's interesting. I don't know how I feel about any of it.'

'Yes, you do. He is your soul mate.'

Grace's head jerked back. 'He can't be,' she said. 'His family hates me and there're so many other witches who are way prettier than me. I wouldn't even register, not with the taint, not with the shadow of necromancy following me. You forget he was there. It's real to him, not a rumor.'

'That was so long ago. I'm sure it wouldn't weigh with him now.'

'You know, he stood up for me. He snubbed Rose Mason. I don't get it.'

Elena laughed. 'I'm so glad. I'm glad he feels the injustice of their treatment of you. I knew he was a gentleman.'

'You're so confident. You talked to him, didn't you?'

'Yes, we used to be good friends.'

Grace snorted and folded her arms. She heard a

bus's engine straining in the traffic and the toots of horns, then a siren. It had seemed so peaceful before.

Elena patted her on the back. 'I know there are other witches, but there is only one you.'

Grace snorted. 'Oh, that's sweet, but you're delusional.'

Elena jerked her thumb over her shoulder. 'Shall we go home?'

'No. I can't face it.' Grace pointed in the other direction. 'Let's walk along the harbor shore. I need some sea energy to clear my head.'

'Sure, that sounds good.'

Grace hooked arms with Elena and they headed down Mort Street to look at the bay. Harbor lights bathed the dark water like stars, but they did little to soothe the hurt or Grace's confusing array of emotions. Declan wasn't worth thinking about. She should let sleeping warlocks lie and be done with it. With a heavy sigh, she realized she had passed the moment she had both longed for and dreaded for nearly nine years, and survived.

Declan tried to concentrate on the witches he was introduced to, but his gaze kept returning to the spot where she had stood. It was as if he could still see her, feel her presence. That ghost of hers that had haunted him since he'd left Sydney so long ago.

'This is Freya, Declan. Declan?' His father elbowed him.

Declan brought his head round. 'Sorry. It's been a long day. Jet lag and all that.' That wasn't a complete lie. He was still adjusting to the new time zone. He could have spelled himself, but then again he'd miss the slow glide into his new life.

Freya was short and well-rounded, with an open face full of freckles. 'I'm pleased to meet the famous Declan Mallory.'

Declan's smile froze. His parents had been telling everyone who stood still long enough that he was a champion battle mage. His father saw his look. 'I'm not famous really.' He coughed. 'Er...Dad. There's Mum. Oh dear, she looks tired. Why don't you check on her?'

His father took the hint.

'I'm sorry about that. I have proud parents who tend to embellish my accomplishments.'

Freya smiled. 'You're too modest. Most of us have read about your exploits. You know, home boy in a foreign place and all that.' She moved a bit closer and her smile widened. 'Did you really battle against members of a dark coven in York?'

His cheeks burnt. 'I was involved in that skirmish. Nothing major.' He felt like a prize bull on display. It had been this way the whole night, women sizing him up as if he was to be their last meal.

'Nothing major?' She flapped a hand. 'Well it's nice to know we have someone like you around if there is any trouble. Although, we only have one dark witch in the north to worry about. Not a whole coven.'

He ran his fingers through his hair. 'Exactly.'

She rubbed up against him. 'So, I'm free if you're interested in spending some time together. We have a great house along the Georges River. Pool, games room, lots of privacy.' She angled her body so he could see her cleavage. She was a buxom woman, and lusty too, if the energy he detected radiating off her was a sign.

'That's a lovely invitation.'

She ran her hand down his forearm and she sent a

potent blast of lust at him. 'I'm serious, Declan. I can be a lot of fun, if you know what I mean.'

'I do.' He coughed, feeling a bit hot. It had been a while since he'd indulged and despite Freya's overtures, which he found off-putting, he couldn't help but respond to the lust-laden thrust she sent at him. He swallowed thickly as the image that she sent him of her naked formed in his mind, with mounds of white flesh being squeezed and jostled during the sex act. He lifted his eyebrows. Freya was full on.

Looking around, he saw his father waving. 'Please excuse me, Freya. We need to leave now. My mother is not well.'

'Sure.' She lifted a hand and waved. 'See you around, gorgeous.' He glanced back over his shoulder and caught her checking out his butt. He bolted, thankful for the excuse to leave. The night had turned into a bit of an emotional grind. The unexpected and unearned adoration irked him to the core. As he scanned the room as they left he realized that there weren't that many warlocks around but there were lots of witches. No wonder he was being treated like a trophy bride. There was no way for him to pursue a woman, because they were all bent on pursuing him. Life in Britain hadn't been like this. He'd had affairs, even though his main focus was study, but never was it dished out to him in this fashion.

He reached his father. 'What is she talking about, *famous?*' he said grumpily. He had to nip that in the bud if he could.

'It's nothing.' His father supported his mother by the elbow. 'Can you help?' His mother was in a faint so Declan supported her from the other side. Someone probably said something that upset her.

'Look,' Declan said, giving his father the eye over

his mother's head. 'It didn't sound like nothing. I wish you wouldn't tell people things about me. Let me make my own way.' His parents had returned a year earlier than he had, as he'd been teaching at the college and wanted to complete the year. Now he saw what a mistake that had been. There was a practically a cheer squad waiting for him.

They reached the car and they assisted his mother onto the seat and shut the door. His father swung round, an embarrassed smile on his face. He shrugged. 'We might have mentioned that you excelled in battle magic…er…won a few combats.'

Declan stood stock-still. 'You didn't.' Hitting his palm against his forehead, he added, 'You didn't exaggerate, did you?'

His father's head tilted to one side. 'Maybe just a tad.'

'Great.' No wonder the women were fawning all over him. All except Grace, who was rather put out, if anything, by their encounter. He didn't need fake idolatry, but real friendships. While that wasn't impossible, now his parents had made it a whole lot harder.

'I'll walk home. Okay?'

'Come on, Dec. Don't be like that.'

'I need some air. It's not far. I like walking.'

His father started the car and backed down the driveway.

Declan walked into the hall, ignoring the women who tried to catch his eye and their overzealous mothers, some which stood in his way. She wasn't there. He excused himself and launched himself out the front door.

There was no one lingering outside. He knew she'd gone. The scent of the sea washed over him. He'd take a walk along the harbor. He could almost smell her perfume in the air. As he walked along, his thoughts whirled. Grace. Grace, whose memory had stayed with him all those years...her dark eyes, fathomless, deep, and yet, warm. Her smile, rich. Her humor, infectious. He'd not forgotten her.

He sat on the grass, watching the harbor lights playing on the water and the shadows of a ferry making its way to Circular Quay. Letting out a sigh, he knew that Grace had not forgotten him either, which was interesting, considering she hadn't sent out any lures and had acted as if she were indifferent to him. Despite that, she knew how long to the day he'd been gone. That told him a different story. She cared, or at least she had.

He didn't think coming home would be like this—causing his emotions to whirl and writhe. He thought he knew what he wanted, where he wanted to be. His family meant a lot to him. They'd suffered enough.

He climbed to his feet and wandered home. His mother would worry until she saw him. You're the only light in my life, my son, she'd say every day. Still did.

When he walked through the door, she turned her head, the lines of worry leaving her brow and mouth. 'Are you all right, Mom?'

'I'm fine,' she said in a weak voice. 'Just tired now.' She put her cup of tea on the bench and came forward. 'So did you meet any interesting witches tonight?'

His father walked in from the living room. 'Oh, he met plenty,' his father chimed in before Declan could answer.

Declan chuckled at his father's enthusiasm. His parents talked about the witches he'd met, about their families and their connections. His eyes rolled up. He knew they were keen to see him settle down, see him choose a mate and reproduce right away. He'd have to break it to them gently that he had other plans, wanted to take his time. Then he noticed there was one woman they didn't speak about. *Grace*. Someone they'd never approve of being his mate, or of him even talking to her. Her being a supposed necromancer was one big part of it. Her being the daughter of Elvira Denholm was the other. He wasn't sure of the history between the two families. He'd been allowed to associate with Grace when he was young, mostly because he was too energetic to keep in the house and his father had allowed it to smooth relations in the coven. He'd seen Grace almost daily —until that dreadful incident. Now he was back and the old prejudice lingered. He'd have to work the truth out of his parents. Besides general talk about bad blood, dark magic and necromancy, nothing specific had ever been mentioned in his hearing, but he guessed there was more to it.

'Up for a nightcap?' his father asked.

'No, thanks. I'm going to turn in.'

His mother limped down the hall to her bedroom.

'See you in the morning.' His father patted him on the back, then leaned in close to whisper, 'Don't mention the Riordon girl to your mother. She doesn't know she was invited—didn't see her.'

Declan sighed. 'Dad.' Rather than argue, he nodded and slipped into his room.

In his bed, he found it hard to sleep. Maybe it was jet lag and maybe it was that his mind was full of thoughts, emotions and memories. It was her smile that kept hovering in his mind and the joyous sound of her laugh that echoed there. It was exquisite torture. *Grace*.

That day when she'd brought back the cat loomed large in his memory. Frightened of what she'd done, he'd bolted and told his parents. He couldn't see that he'd done wrong in that, but the consequences were severe. After that day, he'd never seen her again.

He rolled over and punched his pillow, trying to make it fit his overgrown shoulders. The hardest and the cruelest thing he'd done that week before he'd left was to ignore her attempts at contact. He'd built a wall around himself so she couldn't touch his mind or hear his thoughts. Perhaps in that, he had done wrong. Maybe.

As he finally drifted off to sleep, he recalled looking into the dark depths of her eyes. There had been hurt there. Lots of hurt. She'd hid it well, but he could see it.

CHAPTER TWO

Grace sat back on the sofa, stroking Fel, an odd sensation really because the cat didn't have fur, just a sort of flimsy, greasy substance. She scratched under Fel's chin and the cat's purr intensified.

That's good. More.

The thought plowed into her mind. She blinked. The cat continued to butt against her hand, demanding more attention.

Grace blinked at the cat, then with a screech leapt up, sending the cat into the air to land at her feet. Fel flicked its tail in annoyance and sauntered away.

Hyperventilating, Grace gaped at the spot where the cat had been.

Her mother raced into the room. 'What is it?'

Grace pointed at the departing cat. 'It spoke to me.'

Elvira scoffed and waved her hand in a dismissive gesture. 'Enough with the pranks, already.' She turned to go.

Incredulous, Grace glared at her mother. 'I'm not pranking. I tell you, it thought at me.'

Elvira snorted and headed to the kitchen. Pausing

in the doorway, she looked back and asked, 'So what did the cat say? What does a cat say, for goddess' sake?'

A bit calmer now, Grace took her seat back on the sofa and tugged her hair behind her ear. 'It said what I was doing was good and asked for more.' A glance at her mother revealed she didn't understand. With a shrug, she added, 'I was scratching her under the chin.'

The rolling of Elvira's eyes forewarned her of her mother's disbelief. 'Really, Grace? Can't you think up something more original?'

She disappeared down the hall.

'I'm not making it up.' Grace stood and yelled after her. 'I can't help it if Fel has a limited vocabulary. It's a cat.'

Her mother halted and swung around, eyebrow raised.

'What do they like?' Grace continued. 'Food, well, she doesn't eat. She's dead. Someone to scratch their itchy bits? That's next on the agenda.'

Elvira turned on her heel. 'I'm very busy now, researching this complex spell. There's no time for frivolity.'

Grace leaned her shoulder on the wall and gave a soft chuckle. 'I'm not being frivolous. Far from it. Don't let me keep you.'

Her mother stood on the threshold to her room, looking at her sideways. 'Are you sure, dear?'

'Yes, fine.' Grace sighed and brushed her fringe out of her face.

'You haven't been yourself since…'

Grace chewed her lip then blew out a breath. 'I'm fine. Forget I said anything. I'm going to find Elena.'

Grace considered that the cat might've spoken to her cousin, and perhaps Elena had forgotten to mention it. She didn't have to read her mother's mind to know that Elvira thought she was losing it. She could picture the beginning of her mother's catalogue of issues now—the stress of seeing Declan Mallory, the reminder of her punishment and continued ostracizm. Well, she wasn't losing it, nor did she want to be an object of pity. So Declan Mallory was back in town. He had the right. It certainly didn't mean that she was losing her grip on reality. The cat spoke, for goddess' sake. Why couldn't her mother accept that?

Grace found Elena in the garden digging up weeds, the burnished copper of her hair tied up in a loose ponytail. She was wearing green capri pants and a white linen shirt. Elena brushed the dirt off her hands as she listened. 'No. I don't think Fel's spoken to me,' Elena replied. 'But then again, I'm not as strong and as talented as you.'

'I don't think that comes into it. The talent comes from the cat.' Grace found a patch of grass and plonked herself down. 'At least you don't think I'm deranged, like Mother.'

Elena dug her trowel into the dirt again. 'It's an undead cat. Who knows what it's capable of? It's not like there's a model.'

'Yes, you're right there.' Grace studied Elena, noting her cousin's mood was low, and tried to think of the cause. She examined what Elena had said and then hit upon it. 'Hey, don't be down on yourself. You have talent, you just have to nurture it.'

'I'm only a half-witch. I'm not going to amount to much.'

'Keep thinking that and you won't. It's your duty to be the best you can be and to explore the limits of your talent. That's the coven rule.'

'Is it?' Elena chewed her lip. 'I don't recall that one.'

'Okay, it's not the rule, but it should be. Don't let other people's attitudes get you down. You have to find yourself and not be bound by other people's expectations.'

'You don't, do you?' Elena sighed and then sat on her heels. 'I wish I had your strength. The things you've had to put up with from the rest of the folk all these years.'

Grace shook her head. 'What choice did I have? I had to keep positive.'

'Yet it hasn't held you back or dampened your spirit. It's like there's a light inside of you, Gracie, and no one can extinguish it.'

Love for Elena surged in Grace's heart. 'Oh Elena, I've had you and Mother to stand beside me, offer comfort. That has helped me through the hard times. But I am what I am and I can't change for them. I can't be what the coven wants because that's not me. I obey the rules because that's the right thing to do, but I'm not going to pretend that I don't have talent just so the rest of the coven can feel safe.

'I don't expect them to embrace me, but I do expect them to accept who and what I am. Well, maybe someday they will.'

Elena wiped the back of her hand across her forehead, leaving a smear of dirt. 'See, you're so together. Me, I'm still a mess, still looking to find who I am and what I want out of life.'

'You'll find it. Hey, I'll leave you to your gardening.' Grace climbed to her feet. 'About Fel, just keep an ear out.' She laughed. 'You know what I mean.'

'I do.' Elena banged the roots of a large weed on the ground to shake off excess dirt before tossing it in the wheelbarrow. 'How are you really, Grace?'

'I'm good.' Grace looked up at the sky, studying a cloud formation. Elena still watched her, but she hoped she wouldn't ask about Declan. The adjustment to him being around again was not going smoothly. She'd thought she had it under control, but her family kept looking at her and offering sympathy and support. She'd thought Declan was all in the past. Dead. Buried. Done. It had been three days since she'd seen him and it was like someone had ripped a Band-Aid off her heart. It smarted something awful.

'Well, you know I'm here if you want to talk.'

Grace laughed. 'What should we talk about? How tall he is? How handsome he's become, and buff too? Shall we talk about that?'

Elena sat back. 'Grace, that's so unfair. You shouldn't have eavesdropped on your mother and me. We didn't want to hurt your feelings.'

'You didn't hurt them. I agree. He's all those things, but he's not for me. You don't understand. We could never rekindle what we had. Besides, we were so young and innocent. We formed a bond. It's all forgotten now.'

'Don't be so sure.'

'Look, he has his pick of witches in the coven. Even if he did fancy me, which he doesn't, I'd be stupid to think it was possible. I've been shunned. His family hates me. Now that's something I wish I didn't overhear.' Grace brushed off her pants. 'I'm going shopping in Balmain. Want to come? I can wait.'

'I'd love to but I promised Elvira I'd go visiting with her. She is working on a spell to help Jane Kranscomes' knees.'

Graced nodded and checked she'd dusted the dirt off her backside. 'Fine then. I'll see you at dinner.'

For some reason Balmain was full of witches that afternoon. Grace had seen four young witches in the first ten minutes of being on Darling Road. She ducked into a boutique to hide from one of them. It was bad enough mingling with the folk when the coven celebrated rights and held events, but casually was even worse. She never knew what to expect. As she saw another witch across the street she pulled back into the store. What were they doing here? One witch who lived locally in Balmain would be considered normal, but unlucky for Grace. The ones she'd spotted were from further afield.

The image of Declan Mallory sprung into her mind. Surely not. She shook her head. They couldn't all be there for him, could they? But that made sense. It was one of the local shopping areas for the Mallorys. He must be in Balmain at the moment too. Grace smiled at the thought. The poor man was being stalked and hunted. The pressure wasn't going to let up until he succumbed to one of the witch's lures. How uncomfortable it must be to have every single witch on the lookout for you, hoping to accidentally-on-purpose bump into you. Well, Declan deserved it for growing up so tall, handsome and buff. She shook her head, pitying those witches. Imagine stooping to such tactics. Where was their pride?

Her standing around doing nothing started to earn her a few odd looks from the other customers. She turned and started flicking through the dresses on the rack with a determination that kept the young shop assistant away. Her heart wasn't really in it but she put on a good show. Nothing really caught her eye and she soon grew bored.

Yet she didn't want to be caught in the street by the witches who had decided they liked shopping in

Balmain all of a sudden. There was a café two doors down. Perhaps she could secure a nice out-of-the-way table where she could brood in peace. As much as she loved her family, some time alone with no one trying to cheer her up or take her mind off things sounded like a plan. It was time to brood—a luxury she wanted to indulge in.

Checking that there were no more witches on the prowl for Declan, she slunk down the street and slipped into the café. Heart set on the rear table, she plowed straight into a tall man on his way out. The zing to her senses made her gasp and jerk back. Looking up, she almost passed out. It was Declan Mallory himself. Her mouth fell open.

'Grace? I'm sorry. So clumsy of me.'

It took a moment before she found her voice. Opening and shutting her mouth a few times helped. 'Oh, no.' She swallowed. 'It…it was my fault. I wasn't looking.'

He relaxed his stance and smiled. 'No. I should have been more careful. I hope I didn't injure you.'

Grace shook her head, unable to form a sentence. Of all the people to run into…

'Have you come here for a coffee? I hear they have a good selection of speciality blends,' he asked, making eye contact.

Dumbly, Grace nodded, her face heating. 'I was… er…heading for that table over there.' It had just been vacated. 'Excuse me. I better go grab it before it gets taken.'

She made it past him as he stepped out of her way.

'May I join you?'

Grace paused and looked over her shoulder. 'Oh, sure. Ah…fine.' She faced the back wall so he couldn't see her face. Her heart beat so fast she thought she was going to faint. *Oh goddess. Be calm. Be collected. People will talk, that is all. He's just being polite. You can deal with that.*

In the back of the café, she took the upholstered booth seat and Declan pulled out the vinyl and chrome chair opposite, ending up with his back to the street. He was wearing a snug pale blue T-shirt that hugged his pecs and sculpted biceps. His strong hands were resting on the table-top, the fingers loosely threaded together. He was wide enough to block out her view of the street. A quick glance at his pale face, and she saw that he was giving her a frank appraisal. He noticed her looking and smiled.

That smile lit a little tongue of flame along her nerve endings. 'It's good to see you, Grace.'

Grace was doing her best to dampen her reaction to him. He was attractive. She was not immune to his physical attributes, the same attributes that had four witches prowling the streets of Balmain. 'Imagine running into you here. I would have thought Rozelle, down the road, more your thing.'

Declan blushed. 'Er…it was a little crowded up there today.'

Grace's tried to look around him to the street. 'Do you mean there's a surplus of witches on the streets in Rozelle as well? I saw at least four here in Balmain.'

Declan's expression became flat, his eyelids lowered. 'Actually there are five here at the moment. Some are quite close.'

It rankled that he'd included her in the count. She was not on the hunt for him. 'Oh well, that's what you get when you let it be known you're looking for a mate.'

He straightened his shoulders, his dark eyes flashing. 'I didn't—I'm not.'

'You're not?' Grace rubbed her chin. 'But I heard—'

He grinned sheepishly and lifted a shoulder. 'Yeah, my folks are kind of keen for me to settle down. I guess they broadcast the news, but they didn't really consult me about it.'

'So what are you doing here? You know, back in Australia?'

Declan relaxed back into his chair. 'Well, my battle training was over in England and I'm a qualified teacher now. I intend to start a small school, teach the young ones fighting skills. My application is being considered by the council.'

'Not to give offense or anything like that, but why do we need to train for battle? I mean, we blend in with humans. We've been peaceful with the other folk for five hundred years.'

'You haven't heard about the dark witch revolt?'

'Yes.' She shrugged. 'But that's in the UK and Europe. The biggest problem we've had here is some of our own leaving the coven and making a new one up north, and that was ages ago, before we were born. Seems to me it's a free world, and if people want to form a new coven they should be able to. I've only ever heard rumors of a dark witch in the north, but no real evidence. If she exists, she must be pretty tame.'

Declan was about to argue, she guessed, but shrugged instead. 'You know, battle training is not all about fighting wars or battles. It's about skills— learning new ones, honing them. It works to curb some aggressive tendencies, too. You may not know it but we've lost a number of our kind to random violence.' He jerked his thumb over his shoulder. 'Out there. On the streets. Being able to protect yourself from harm is a skill every witch or warlock should have.'

'There's more to it, isn't there?'

Twin points of color grew on his cheeks. 'No. Forget I mentioned it. Let's just say it's good to be prepared.'

Grace tilted her head, considering his words. She'd not been paying attention to what was going on overseas, but she intended to now. If there was something to be wary of, she wanted to be across it. 'I see your point. I did hear a rumor that you were rather good.'

His high cheekbones were accentuated by the blush that spread over his face. 'My parents are too ready to sing my praises.'

She chuckled lightly. 'They love you. You've done a lot to make them proud. Nothing to be ashamed of.'

The waiter came over and took their order. 'So what do you do with your time? A powerful witch like you, the whole world would be for the taking.'

Grace lowered her head and stared at her fingers, which she was tying in knots. 'About that.'

'Do you mean you're not working for the coven?'

'Yes, well. I...er...help out in the preschool two days a week.'

'What?' He threw himself back in his seat. His dark eyes studied her face. 'That's such a waste.'

'As a volunteer.' She struggled to maintain eye contact. While she hadn't relaxed in his presence, there had been a certain rapport. Now, with this line of questioning, uneasiness grew. She fought for a balance in her emotions. She was happy with the status quo. There was no way she would be intimidated by him just because he disagreed.

He thumped his fist down on the table, making her start. 'I can't believe that they could be so stupid, to waste your talent like that. There is so much good you could be doing.' He balled his hand into a fist. For the first time in nine years, she reached out with her senses, brushing them against his aura gently so that he wouldn't detect her. It was enough of a contact for her to know he was genuinely upset for her.

'I don't hold grudges. That day changed—'

He leaned forward so that she had nowhere else to look but at him. 'Do you blame me, Grace?'

She shook her head. 'Of course not.' Her denial was instinctive. She had never blamed him. It had been her own stupid fault.

'I ran and tattled on you.'

'My mother would have called the council anyway, reported the incident. You know a ghost cat is not easy to hide. It would have come out.'

'But I never saw you again.' That comment cut into her heart.

She swallowed and stared at the table-top. She did not want him to know how much that had hurt. 'You did the right thing. Please can we not—' The memory of that day flashed up. Grace squashed it; she didn't want to relive that day. She'd lost her best friend —*him*. That was the worst of it. She'd done something miraculous that she'd never regretted, despite it being so wrong. Dark witches raised the dead. Not good ones. But Elena kept her cat. Grace had been punished and learnt later why it was such a terrible thing.

'Please, Grace, let me speak. You don't understand. I never got a chance to talk to you again, never got the chance to say how sorry I am. I've thought about it. It's been in my mind since I saw you. It was my fault. It wouldn't have happened but for me.'

'No, that's not—'

He squeezed her hand. It was as if he had shocked

her with a bolt of electricity. She froze, breath still in her lungs, until he moved his hand away again. And then, like the breath was running out of her, she sagged.

'I was annoyed at Elena. She kept clinging to Fel and I wanted her to play tennis with me. I grabbed the cat off her, scared it so it ran onto the road straight in front of a passing motorcycle. I caused her beloved pet to die.'

Grace narrowed her eyelids. She couldn't believe this. He'd been harboring guilt all this time. She'd never suspected his part in it. 'Elena never said anything. I don't know what to—'

'I'm just as much at fault as you. I knew Elena loved Fel; that she was still adjusting to her new life with your family. I knew, knew how much you loved her.'

'You knew everything about me.' There, she'd said it. Alluded to their bond.

'Yes, Grace. I did. I remember all of it.'

The coffees arrived. Grace's emotions churned. Anger, hurt and regret jumbled together. These were feelings she wanted to avoid. She was in the café to hide from it all, not confront it. The past. The future. Yet, she couldn't escape. Declan Mallory was here, tossing it at her as if he were tossing stones in a deep pond. He was guilty? Give her a break. He didn't reach through the veil of death and bring a spirit back. He hadn't known she could do that. No one had. What right did he have to feel guilty about that day? He'd done the right thing. If only...if only...he hadn't gone away, but that wasn't his choice, was it?

Her coffee spilled when she stood up abruptly. 'I'm going. Something has come up.' She fumbled for coins in her pocket and tossed them on the table. Tugging her bag onto her shoulder, she angled around the tables. Near running, she made it to the street and then jogged along until she found another boutique to hide in.

Once inside, colors assaulted her. She flicked through the clothes blindly, just for something to do. Why had he bailed her up? Why had he brought up the past? The past she had to live with every day. A few deep breaths and calm returned. He must have thought she was a nut, running out like that.

It was all too hard to put straight. Declan messed with her head. No, it was her heart. He was a beacon of energy that her spirit craved. Had been since that day when they had melded their minds, their spirits and their essences. Declan had experienced the very core of her. He was a bright, warm essence that bathed and penetrated her. Later, Declan had said that not many of the folk could make such a connection. It was a rare thing. Something only the ancient texts talked about. They shared a bond. A bond now severed. She'd never let herself get that close to anyone again. She doubted they could do it again if they tried. That melding had happened because they were young and innocent. There were no barriers; no built-up hurt or mistrust to prevent it.

Someone was watching her. Her head came up and the vibration tickled the back of her tongue. It was a witch. Surreptitiously she angled around, checking the mirror. It was Danila. Although she was ostensibly examining a dress, Grace could feel the bad vibe leaking from the other woman. Had she seen her with Declan or was it general dislike? Grace remembered the woman's slight from the other night. Right now, Grace couldn't deal with petty distain. She had other more pressing issues on her mind.

Slipping through the other customers, she made

for the door. A wave of magic rippled around her—a spell of some kind. She was almost at the door. The door alarm went off. Then suddenly, Declan loomed in front of her.

Dumbfounded, Grace hesitated near the door. She backed up as Declan came into the store. 'What?'

Declan looked at her shoulder bag. Following the direction of his gaze, she saw that there was a blouse sticking out of the opening. The shop assistant came bounding up. 'Miss? Are you going to pay for that?'

'I…er…' Grace threw her glance around the store. *Danila. That cow. Where did she get to?* A change room curtain rippled at the back of the shop.

She swung back around, remembering Declan was there. Why did he have to see this embarrassing incident? Would he even believe she was innocent?'

'Darling,' he began with a tender smile. 'Let me see that blouse.' He tugged it from her shoulder bag. 'So nice of you to bring it over for me to have a look at. I'm sorry I had to slip out for a sec.' He turned to the shop assistant. 'I'm sorry we set the alarm off.'

He held the blouse up. It was hideous. He hoped he didn't make her buy it. 'It's not your color.' He leaned over and kissed her on the check. Grace shut down her senses. He could not see into her; she would not let him in. That was an intimacy only children could afford.

He passed the garment back to the shop assistant. 'I saw a much better one in a shop down the road. Come on.'

He linked arms with her and led her out of the shop. Grace's heart thumped. Her head span. When they were out on the street, he angled her out of the pedestrian flow. 'Oh goddess. What are you doing?' She drew back her arm. 'Were you following me?'

'Yes, I was.'

Grace gaped and clicked her mouth shut. 'The nerve of you.'

His glared in the direction of the shop. 'Are you going to report her?'

'What?'

He brought those dark eyes of his back to her face. She saw that he had green flecks around his irises. His eyes were hazel, not brown. 'Are you going to report Danila What's-Her-Face for what she did?'

Grace lowered her eyebrows and stepped around him. He followed close behind. Damn, why wouldn't he leave her alone? She swung about around, confronted him. 'What's the point in that? It won't change anything. Retaliation only makes it worse.'

She hitched her bag higher and turned to go. After two steps, his hand was on her shoulder.

'But what she did was wrong.' He spun her around so they faced each and then leaned in. 'It could have gotten messy in there. You have to fight back.' They were almost nose-to-nose.

Grace shook her head. 'I can deal with it. I was distracted. Normally...'

'I upset you, didn't I?'

She dropped her gaze. 'Not at all.'

'At least do me the courtesy of being truthful.'

He tugged her out of the path of a bunch of school kids. Leaning in close, he spoke into her ear. 'I didn't set out to make you feel bad—'

'I didn't think you would.'

'Please let me finish, Grace. I had to get that off my chest, that little secret I've carried all these years. It took a load off my mind—'

'That's great for you.' Now he was making her angry.

'Please, Grace. I didn't think that it would hurt—'

'What do you know about it? Oh, precious son returned from triumph. What could you possibly know about my life?'

'Grace, I'm sorry. Forgive me; I'm a stupid dick. I—'

'I've got to go.'

She put some distance between them but he followed her with long strides, dodging other pedestrians. He caught her in the car park. 'Grace, wait.' He grabbed her arm and swung her around.

'Please stay away from me. Just pick one of the numerous witches dying to have your baby and stay out of my life.' She took a few steps, keeping her back to him when he spoke.

'Grace. That's not fair. You've got to give me a chance.'

She swung around. 'No, I don't. You had your chance and you blew it.'

Declan snorted. 'I was fifteen, Grace. Give me a break. You say you can deal with it, have dealt with it, but you're still that thirteen-year-old girl, too ignorant to see what she's doing.'

'Go away!'

'No. I won't. I was a child. I deserve—no, I demand a second chance.'

Grace clenched her jaw and stormed away. After a few angry steps, she readjusted her shoulder bag, hauling it onto her shoulder, and ran.

The house was empty when she arrived home. She stood in the hallway, realizing her mother and Elena were still out. She took great satisfaction in slamming the front door, then she threw up the house wards and stomped into her room. She tossed her bag at the wall and then flopped down on the bed. After banging her head against the mattress a few times, she dragged a pillow under her and let the tears flow. All those hurtful things he'd said were like lashes across her heart. He was wrong. She'd grown up from that young girl who had idolized him. She saw him now for the conceited jerk he was. Let all the single witches in the coven hound him to the ground. Let him mate with every single one. He probably had the stamina. As a bystander, she'd have a crack-up time laughing at them all.

CHAPTER THREE

'All right then,' Grace said, then clapped her hands when the children didn't look to her. 'We are making scones with a little something extra in them.' She caught one young boy's attention. 'Earl, what are we putting in the scones today?'

Earl was five years old with a mass of dark ringlets. He tilted his head. 'Love!'

Grace nodded. 'Yes, love.'

'Esme? What kind of love are we adding to our mixture?'

Esme did a hair toss. She was six and the oldest of this group. 'Familial love.' She looked down at Earl. 'So our families will feel our love through our food.'

Grace nodded. 'Yes, it's a simple basic spell. What are our rules with spells?'

A hand shot up. 'Yes, Wade.'

'Only for family. No humans.'

'Yes, that's right. None of the scones are for non-folk, because that wouldn't be right.'

The children combined their ingredients and she came around and helped them add the essential ingredient, the spell that would activate it. Technically, if a human ate the scone they would be no more affected than one of the folk. It was a basic potion spell, with very little effect. The children would earn extra cuddles and the family would have a warm, tender evening. It was part of the coven's curriculum for the children in the coven. She paused by Madison's desk. The young girl, with her hair slicked into a bun, chewed her lips thoughtfully. 'Is there something wrong?'

The young girl's hazel eyes turned to her. 'I think I did it wrong.'

'Let me see.' Grace knelt down and probed the pile of dough with her senses. 'Mmm. An extra portion of orange blossom in there is amplifying the spell bindings. Don't worry. We can start afresh.'

Madison pouted prettily. 'But Miss Grace…'

'It won't take long, promise.'

Grace disposed of the dough, zapping it quickly as it hit the bin. Soon after, she had her young pupil mixing up a new batch and assisted her with the spell. Madison's smile made what she was doing so satisfying. The coven may be wary of her, but Grace loved working with the children.

A loud bang made her start. 'What the…?'

She walked over to the full-length windows that looked out over the playground. *Wham*, a ball headed straight at her, then diverted at the last second. Grace had jumped back and her pupils laughed.

'That was entertaining, wasn't it?' She turned her back on the goings on outside and faced her class. 'Now, are our ovens at the right temperature?' She walked along, checking the temperature gauges, and adjusted one or two.

Through the window she saw the older kids forming lines. The ball was obviously forgotten. She wondered what they were up to, but had to concentrate on getting everyone's scones in the oven.

While the scones were baking, the pupils put away their things and cleaned all the utensils while Grace locked up the potion ingredients in the cupboard. The children outside were growing rowdy. There was high-pitched cheering over the deeper male voice. The intermediate grade had a new teacher, obviously.

The goings on outside gradually distracted her pupils. Grace sighed as she watched them filter away from their tables. Grace clapped her hands again when all her pupils were lined up along the windows watching what was going on outside. 'Come on, you lot. Have a look in the oven. There're some lovely scones there.'

Only a few of the children peeled away from the windows. 'Only a few more minutes until break. Who wants to miss out on seeing what's going on outside?'

A few heads turned. 'Come on, see to your scones and then you can go outside to play.'

Most of her class went to check their ovens and the aroma of freshly-baked scones filled the air. A few straggler boys needed extra prompting.

'Now wrap them all up in your damp tea towels.'

'Can we use magic to do that?' Esme asked.

'Of course, if you can manage it.'

Grace scratched her chin and studied the ceiling while Esme attempted to tie the tea towel in an elaborate bow. It was never going to work. It wasn't that Esme didn't have the talent, but due to the tea towel not having enough length. Eventually Esme worked it out, picking up the cloth and examining it. With a nod to herself, she tried again, making a neat knot. Sometimes children had to learn through trial and error rather than being told. Within reason, of course. Dangerous activities should be carefully explained to avoid disasters. Grace had learned the hard way about that.

'Outside, the lot of you.' Grace chuckled as she watched them race to the doorway and squeeze themselves through five at a time. Only experience would teach them. Grace kept an eye out for shoving or injuries, but after a few minutes, they'd sorted themselves out into an orderly line and charged outside, yelling and screaming with joy at being set free.

Grace checked the classroom, restoring order so the next teacher could start afresh. Papers and pens aligned themselves on the desks. Rubbish popped into bins. Chairs tucked themselves under desks. With a smile, she quelled her magic and went to see how the children were faring outside.

When she got outdoors, the children were nowhere to be seen. Slightly startled, she scanned the field and listened hard. It didn't take long for her to locate the children who were all crowded into the arena, a small area set aside for people to watch games of basketball or handball. As she walked up she had an uncomfortable churning in her stomach, because the new teacher looked remarkably like Declan Mallory. In the shadow of the tiered seating, she chewed her lips. It was Declan, and he was teaching the children a targeting game.

As the school had a privacy ward none of the neighbors would be able to see exactly what the children were doing, which was good. Precautions like that kept the coven invisible to non-folk, kept the peace.

At first she was annoyed that Declan was teaching them battle skills. She didn't think it was really necessary. They had lived in peace for so long; why incite the folk to violence?

Yet as she watched on she changed her mind. The intermediate class was using magic to thrust little pellets through a target hole. The children watching roared with laughter as some of the pellets went wide and hit Declan in the butt. Other misguided pellets pinged the top of people's heads, or stung their arms and legs.

Declan appeared to be shielding most of the children so that none were harmed. She was quite impressed by that feat because it required a lot of concentration to use magic in a number of ways simultaneously. There were about fifteen rowdy students he was supervising too.

Grace could see that the target practice was helping the young witches and warlocks to hone their skills. It was rather an innocent game, but not all folk could manipulate matter so she looked around, seeing what he had those students doing. Declan had the students tossing pellets with their hands and then others guiding the missiles into the target with their talent. That way everyone was equal whether they were propelling the missile with their magic or guiding it.

Guiding took a lot less work because the throw gave the pellet its momentum. Grace looked around at her class sitting on the tiered seats and wondered at how engrossed they were in the proceedings before them. She knew they enjoyed her cooking classes but she could see that they really got something worthwhile from his game tactics.

While she didn't agree with Declan's view on battle readiness, she could definitely learn from his approach, and she began thinking of ways to make some of her classes more fun by using games.

'Grace?'

Grace straightened her posture, doing her best not to blush at being caught out watching him. 'Er...hi.'

'Okay everyone, lesson's over. Go take a break,' Declan called out to his class and then navigated through the swarm of children who were making their way to hand toss the missiles or run around the field. Grace watched as her class climbed down and ran off to play with the others, leaving her alone to face Declan.

'I didn't know you were teaching today,' Declan said as he came up to her, smiling, the sunlight twinkling in his eyes.

'It wasn't a secret. I didn't expect you'd be teaching here. I thought you were setting up your own school.' Grace hadn't forgiven him for the other day, but she was polite. Having been snubbed so often, she couldn't bring herself to do it to others.

'I have to begin somewhere. The coven school was the natural place to start.'

She nodded. 'I see.' She made her comment sound bored.

Declan stood with his feet apart and rubbed a hand through his hair. He squinted into the afternoon sun. 'I guess I deserved that.'

She jolted. 'I don't know what you mean.'

He shook his head. 'Can't we call it a truce? I mean, I know I upset you the other day in Balmain, but I wasn't trying to.'

Grace glowered. 'Well, I'd hate to see you trying to upset me then.' She resisted rolling her eyes. That sounded so churlish.

He grimaced. 'I said I deserve a second chance—'

'Actually, *demanded* was the word that stuck in my mind.' He was trying hard, and she wasn't as nearly upset with him as she'd thought she'd be. Perhaps all those tears had been therapeutic.

Declan winced as he studied her face. 'Look, how about after we finish up here, we go and have a picnic.'

'A picnic?' Her eyes narrowed.

He smiled wider. 'I know a nice place.'

'I don't think—' She could think of no reason, other than she'd hate people talking about her, linking her name with his.

'Come on. What do you have to lose? Some time?'

'Er…I have…' She had nothing else on.

'Please, Grace.'

She rolled her eyes. It was very hard to ignore him, with that sparkling gaze and that smile. Her resistance crumbled. What did she have to lose? Her heart was armored up. All she needed to do was enjoy the view. Maybe having people talk about them would give her some revenge, scatter the feed among the chickens. The bitch-witches would go wild. Her mouth curled up in a smile and she broke eye contact. 'Well…okay.'

'Do you mind riding pillion on a motorbike?'

'A motorbike?' A thrill rushed through her. 'A ride on a bike. How exciting!'

'It's new.' He studied her face.

'Awesome. I've never been on one, new or old.'

Declan grinned and put his hands on his hips, his gaze ranging out over the children. 'You finish up now, don't you? Preschool usually finishes early.'

'Yes.'

'Shouldn't be too long now before the parents arrive to collect your little darlings.'

'You forget. You were once a little darling.'

He winked at her. 'I still am. I'm due to hand over

to the next teacher after the break, so we can set off then.'

Grace walked over to the target with Declan following behind. 'Do you mind if I have a go at this?'

'I thought you didn't approve of battle training.'

She grinned. 'I don't. But this is useful for honing skills, no matter what you're aiming for. I don't think I've tried a game like this before. You'll have to be kind.'

Declan chuckled. 'Sure, I can do that. Shall we compete or keep it friendly?'

Grace took in the scatter of plastic pellets on the ground, noticing that there were two different colors. 'Definitely competitive.'

'You're sure?'

'You bet. You're on.'

With a click of his fingers, the pellets ordered themselves into two piles. 'The object is to get as many pellets through the target hole as you can in the shortest space of time. They have to pass through the hole in the target, not around. The first one to get all of their colored pellets through wins.'

Grace nodded and folded her arms. 'That sounds simple enough. Ready?'

Her pile of pallets rose into the air, all neatly ordered in a line. Declan did a double take upon seeing it.

'I thought you said—'

Grace's pellets began to move. Declan quickly gathered his and formed them into a swarm, all circling, ready to thrust themselves through the small target hole.

Grace tilted her head to the side. Without looking at the target, her missiles shot through one by one. Declan's pellets couldn't compete, being knocked out of the way by the speed of hers. With a grunt, she felt a shift in his power and he aimed his pellets at hers, knocking them from their path. Pellets began flying in all directions as they shot through the air, ricocheting off one another.

It became a battle between them rather than a battle to get the missiles through the target. The sounds of laughter reached their ears. They had an audience as their pellets continued dancing in a halo, surrounding them from the ground to well above their heads. With a lift of her eyebrow, Grace channelled her pellets into the target opening using about ten to protect her line. He was good, but Grace was better. She was sending his pellets further afield on different trajectories and he had to use more magic to bring them back. His pellets raced back with speed and force that would hurt if they impacted on skin.

A glance at his face, and she could see that it was a strain for him. Sweat beaded on his brow and he chewed his lip. He had underestimated her. She grinned and then her smile froze. His gaze was not centered on her but he had a faraway look as he stretched his senses out across the field, propelling his pellets as he did.

The cheering grew louder. 'Come on, Miss Riordon,' shouted the children from her class.

'Come on, Mr Mallory. Squash her!' came the chant from his students.

Grace only had a few pellets left and was set to win. Her smile was wide and then suddenly dropped when Declan grabbed her to him. Not quite registering what he was about, she was stunned when he tilted her backward and kissed her. His hot mouth captured hers and he went for it, sending his tongue to tease her own. Her mind went blank but her mouth was on automatic, responding to the kiss. Totally distracted, her pellets fell to the ground, while his rammed through the hole, ripping the target in the process. The cheers turned to yells and catcalls. Declan had won.

He lifted his head away, yet kept his arms around her. She pushed her hands against his chest, and then wiped his kiss from her mouth. 'Of all the mean tricks…that's cheating.' She was appalled at his tactics. How could he kiss her like that and still concentrate on his pellets? It was downright insulting.

Declan grinned from ear to ear. 'Fair is fair. I underestimated you but I found a way to even the score.'

Grace tossed her head back. 'That won't happen again,' she said and then stormed off, highly outraged. The children were still cheering. She shook her head. That piece of gossip would be all over the coven in a couple of hours.

'We'll see about that,' Declan called after her. Grace wanted to flip him the bird, but didn't as the parents had started to arrive to pick up their children. Esme's mother waved to her. 'How was the scone making?' she called.

Grace put a smile on her face. 'They did well. Let me unlock the classroom and you can see for yourself.'

After tramping back to the classroom she opened the door, letting the children fetch their cloth-wrapped parcels, and she cheerfully chatted to the parents while they waited. As she took her time with each parent, she secretly hoped that Declan would have left already and she would be saved the embarrassment of telling him to get lost. She had no intention of riding pillion and heading off on a picnic with Declan I-always-have-to-win Mallory.

It was hard to keep smiling when her teeth grated. The nerve of him, to use that tactic…and she'd fallen for it, like one of his bitch-witches would. What she couldn't figure out was whether she was more injured by him beating her or by the fact that he could kiss her and still concentrate on other things. Her fist clenched and then Earl came up to her. 'Here is a scone for you, Miss.'

Grace's heart softened. Earl was so cute with his mop of curls and dark brown eyes. 'That's so nice of you.' She took the proffered scone. 'Thank you.'

Thinking that enough time had elapsed for Declan to have taken off, Grace chased up the remaining children, who were telling their parents how they made the scones and what so-and-so had done.

The last child left. With a sigh, Grace surveyed the empty classroom. Everything was in its proper place. She could no longer stall by lingering there. She had to go outside and either hope he was gone or deal with him being there.

Only her car remained in the car park. The sun had dropped lower in the sky so that dappled light fell across her car, a little red VW Golf. It was a lovely spring day in Sydney. The crunch of gravel behind her made her spin round. Declan stood there in a black leather jacket, holding a spare helmet in one hand. 'Here you go,' he said, passing it to her.

'Do you expect me to go with you after what you just did?'

'Of course. You aren't a spoilt sport, are you?'

Grace sucked in an indignant breath. 'You cheated.'

'No, I didn't. In battle you must expect the unexpected.'

Grace spluttered. She hadn't thought of that. 'You can go jump—'

'I'm parked near the entrance.' He jerked his head to one side, indicating the front of the school.

He was being so polite and ignoring her outrage. Grace chewed her lip. He'd been reasonable when pointing out her failure. It was true. She'd lost because he'd managed to distract her. She lifted her chin, not liking that he might be right.

There had been no expectation that she'd had a chance to beat him at his own game. She wasn't a sore loser; that wasn't it. It was because he'd kissed her and totally drew her into his moment and away from hers. That was what annoyed her, the fact that he had power over her. She did not want that. Right then, she didn't want to fight anymore. She had to relax and let all that tension go. Declan was back in her world and she had to deal with it as best she could.

Declan held the helmet out to her again. Casting her doubts away, she took it and put it on her head. 'Right then, let's test out this bike of yours.'

Declan grinned and then turned away, leaving her to follow. She didn't mind so much. There was something to be said about not fighting it, as she could enjoy the man Declan had become. It was only a picnic. The view was rather good. As he walked, his leather jacket hung from his wide shoulders and his dark blue denim hugged his butt cheeks. They were very squeezable. That made her grin to herself. *I bet he would find that thought disconcerting.* She filed that one away for later use.

The bike came into view. It was retro looking, with a curvy red petrol tank and cool spoke wheels. Its chrome exhaust pipe caught the light. 'Wow.'

He chuckled at her reaction. 'Mmm, exactly. It's a Triumph Speedmaster. All the elegance of an earlier period, but with modern features that make for a great ride. I prefer the upright position; helps with being tall.'

Grace was impressed. The motorbike looked hot. Her attention moved to him. He looked hot in that get-up. Talk about bad-ass hunk status.

Don't go there. Remember the bitch-witches. She repressed a sigh and decided to change the topic.

'You ride that?'

'Sure I do.' He pulled a small jacket out of one of his panniers, holding it up to her. 'That should fit.' He took her handbag and placed it inside.

Grace took the brown leather garment and sniffed it. It smelled new to her. Did he buy it especially? While she did up the jacket, Declan went over his bike. 'I did a lot of touring when I was in Britain,' he said as he squatted down to inspect the engine. 'Lots of narrow roads with hedgerows and tunnels made out of trees, and out-of-the-way woods where you could stretch out and feel the earth beneath you, and hear the birds in the trees and the wind caressing branches and leaves.'

Grace lifted her eyebrows. Declan Mallory was a little bit more earthy than she'd expected. She finished buttoning up her jacket. 'So where are we going on this little picnic?'

Declan straddled the bike, holding the handlebars so that the bike was fully upright and released the kickstand. 'Come on, get on. Hold onto my shoulders and lift your leg over.' Grace did as instructed. He pulled his helmet on. 'Hold me around the waist.'

Grace did up the strap on her helmet. She thumped him lightly on the shoulder and yelled into his ear. 'I said where are we going?'

'The Blue Mountains.' He started the bike, with the noise reaching her through the helmet.

'The Blue Mountains? That's no little picnic. It's too late to go there now.'

Declan revved the motor, giving no indication

that he'd heard a word she'd said. She didn't attempt to mind speak him. That door had closed a long time ago. The bike lurched forward. Grace held on for dear life. She managed to hail her mother and Elena to say she'd be late for dinner and for them not to worry. Her mother sent back a distracted 'okay'. Grace shrugged and held on, resting her face on Declan's broad leather-clad back to hide from the wind.

The journey on the bike exposed her to the elements. Her face was buffeted by hard wind, her body stroked by powerful gusts. She'd never ridden on a bike before and she loved it. Declan's strong body controlled the bike, expertly navigating the traffic along the Great Western Highway that led them up to the mountains. She'd been to Leura before, as a number of the coven lived that far out. They liked the bush setting, the mountain climate, and the small little wooden houses that reeked of old-world charm. It was an easy distance for key festivals and the mountains had their own magical allure. Grace had visited a family there during a series of thunderstorms. Energy had crackled and sizzled around them. She remembered that feeling of being so energized and close to nature, and the raw power that existed in the earth.

By the time they reached Springwood, hunger gained Grace's attention. She hadn't eaten since the morning. She'd left Earl's scone behind. It was then she noticed that Declan didn't appear to have any food with him. She remembered the panniers and if he had food in them, it was very modest indeed. Grace could have eaten several servings of turkey with all the trimmings, her hunger was that bad.

Finally, after zipping through a number of other mountain suburbs, Declan pulled over onto a grass-covered area. 'He we are.' He tugged off his helmet and gestured to a small cottage, obscured by shrubs and a riotous cottage garden.

Grace took off her own helmet and shook out her hair. Using her fingers, she tried to arrange it to get rid of the flattened hair she'd acquired from a couple of hours riding pillion while Declan held the bike for her.

'Where is here?' She lifted her leg off the bike, her muscles stiff.

Opening the pannier, he pulled out her handbag, passing it to her.

She stretched and shook out her legs. The sun had dropped lower on the horizon. They would have to travel at night to get back home to Balmain. She kept her mouth shut, although she was dying to make a snarky comment about the so-called 'picnic'.

Declan dismounted from the bike and engaged the bike stand. He reached into the panniers and took out what looked like a bottle of wine wrapped in brown paper, and another shopping bag. Grace watched him with hooded eyelids, suspicious all of a sudden.

'I thought you said we were going on a picnic. That to me implied food and maybe a blanket, a beach, a park or something.'

Declan tossed his keys in the air and caught them. 'Patience. All will be revealed.' He strode past her and stepped onto the veranda of the little house. He paused, looked over his shoulder and said, 'What are you waiting for? You're not a scaredy-cat, are you?'

With a sniff, Grace tossed back her head. 'You would have to try a lot harder to scare me, Mallory.'

She raced to catch up, lifting her chin defiantly when she drew level with him.

'Then enter.' His eyes studied her, pushing the door open.

A warm liquid feeling overshadowed her annoyance. In that moment, for that moment, it was as if they had never been apart, never been separated by terrible deeds.

Then, letting that thought go, she stepped into the house. A warm polished floor greeted her gaze. The short hallway opened onto a cosy lounge room with stuffed sofas in natural-colored beige upholstery, and a fireplace framed with old-fashioned green glazed tiles. A modern kitchen led off the room. Declan strode over and put the bottle on the bench and started opening cupboards and pulling out wineglasses. 'Will you take a glass?'

'Yes, I'd love a drink.' Grace ambled around the lounge room. The fireplace was stacked with wood, ready to light. 'Should I start the fire?' It was starting to cool down as the sun disappeared, though it wasn't actually cold.

'If you wouldn't mind. I'll get our picnic ready.'

Grace chuckled to herself as she sent a spark into the kindling. As the wood caught, she shook her head. *Declan Mallory was a trickster.* What was he planning?

Collecting her wine, she took a sip and then sprawled herself on the sofa, drinking in the atmosphere of the cosy little cottage. It really was a relaxing, peaceful place to be. She took another sip of wine and let it slide slowly down her throat. Then she frowned at a sudden thought. *What was she doing alone in the Blue Mountains with Declan Mallory?*

She bolted upright. Declan was slicing bread in the kitchen. She didn't know what to do. It was a bit far to hail her mother, and a tad embarrassing.

Climbing out of the seat, she tugged down her top and shored up her courage. Strolling to the kitchen, she leaned against the wall, projecting a calmness she didn't quite feel. Declan was focused on embellishing plates with chicken drumsticks and salad. It was picnic food, but not a picnic place. 'Declan, what is going on? I mean, it's late. How will we get home in time?'

He glanced her way. 'In time for what?'

Grace swallowed, not quite sure how to answer because it would reveal that she was insecure being alone with him, or worse, affected by being alone with him. And that was also presumptuous, because there was no romance between them. She'd made it quite clear she wasn't interested, and she thought he had made it quite clear that it had been her fault all those years ago, and that she should feel sorry for him for the distress it had caused him. But then she realized that she was being a bit hysterical as she hadn't really come to terms with seeing him again, or interpreted all the resulting emotions it had stirred up inside her.

'Well?'

'Oh? Nothing in particular.' She watched him spoon some potato salad onto the plates, losing herself to her thoughts again. In the last few days, she'd calmed a bit—gotten used to the idea of him being around. And while him coming back had stirred up people's memories of her necromancy, it had soon died. People were more interested in him. He had proven himself to be quite a legend while in Britain, battling rebel folk. Yes, she'd looked up the uprising he'd fought in. That was a disturbing incident, but there had been no signs of similar unrest here in Australia, *thank the goddess*, she thought. His parents were proud and had a right to be. She couldn't begrudge him that, even though, at thirteen, the separation had been very hard indeed. Still, events had made her what she was and she wasn't unhappy with that. Declan had done well, too.

'Here we are then.' He passed her a plate. 'Shall we take a seat by the fire?'

With a nod, she followed him to the lounge room. He put his plate on the coffee table and she did likewise, sitting on the opposite end of the couch. The flickering fire sent out warmth to envelope them. Declan had taken off his leather jacket and proceeded to unclip his knee-length boots. He was making himself at home. 'Is this your place then?'

'Yes, I bought it before I came back. As much as I love my parents, I really enjoy my own space. They come out here on the weekends when they want to get away. I think they are tempted to move out here and retire.'

Grace took a bite of chicken and swallowed. 'Witches and warlocks really retire?'

He swallowed a mouthful. 'Not really, no. But I mean retire from the city life. There is a fantastic garden out back. My parents have plans to grow herbs and essential ingredients and supply them to the coven.'

Grace nodded and took another bite of chicken. It tasted delicious. Her hunger was still rampant so she took another drumstick and chomped on it.

'You are hungry.'

Grace nodded and continued to chew. He passed her a napkin. She grabbed it and wiped two fingers, and dabbed around her mouth.

'More wine?' He held up the bottle. Grace lifted her glass.

She was starting to feel more at home. She kicked off her shoes and wiggled her toes in front of the fire. 'This is nice and quiet. I love it.'

'I'm glad you like it.'

Grace picked at her salad and took a bite of bread, washing it down with a couple of mouthfuls of wine. She was starting to feel mellow. No longer wary of Declan, she leaned her head against the back of the couch and breathed deeply, letting the atmosphere sink into her senses.

Declan cleared their plates away and topped up their wine before he sat back down again.

'I'm glad you like the place.'

'Mmm. I do.' Her eyes were closed. Drowsiness climbed up her limbs, stroked her mind.

Declan moved closer. She stayed very still, not quite sure what he was up to. His finger traced along her nose and her eyes snapped open. 'What are you doing?'

'Admiring the view.'

Grace sat up, her back straight. 'Perhaps we should go back now.'

Declan sat back, relaxing into the sofa. 'No, not yet. I think we need to rest a little longer.'

'In that case, you should keep your hands to yourself and maintain your distance. I didn't come here to be seduced by you.'

'Why did you come?'

'You asked me as a peace offering, I thought.'

He lifted an eyebrow. 'Is that the only reason?'

Grace had to think a minute. 'Yes.' She wasn't about to go into her feelings or try to explore them with Declan. It was none of his business.

'I see.' He gazed into her face. 'Well, Grace, I've got some news for you. We're not going back to Balmain tonight.'

Grace chuckled to herself. 'Sure. When did you become such a kidder?'

'I'm not joking.'

Grace slipped off the sofa, putting the coffee table

between them. 'Is this some kind of joke? Because, you know, I've been there done that.'

'You have? With who?'

Grace put their hands to her head. 'Don't go there. I really can't be here alone with you...tonight.'

He stood up and came round the table, capturing her elbows in his hands. 'Why, Grace? What's so special about tonight?'

'Nothing.' She wanted to back away, but he held her gently in his grip. She wasn't prepared for this, not expecting him to want to be alone with her, so far away from everyone else. She didn't know what to do. She'd not been alone with any man. No one in the coven would have anything to do with her during her teens, except to tease her in some way about being a necromancer. Her peers had joked that she'd dated the dead because no live warlock would want to spend time with her.

'Grace.' He spoke her name softly in her ear and his breath brushed against her neck. She shivered. 'Tell me, Grace, what are you thinking? Feeling?'

'I can't. Don't make me.'

'Share it with me. See into me—let me see into you.'

She put space between them, her back now to the fire. 'No. I won't. I—'

'Why, Grace? We used to be close. I know it was a long time ago...we could touch each other again, if you try.'

She shook her head. 'It was a mistake. We were young, innocent. It won't work now. We have too much armor, too much inbuilt protection.'

'Try.'

'No, I can't.'

'Please, Grace. I want this.'

Her gaze lifted to his. 'Want what?'

In the next breath he was there, his hot lips on her neck making her gasp. 'To be close to you, Grace. To share myself with you.' She was caught between wanting to push him away and wanting to surrender. This was Declan, the person who she had been close to once, closer than she had been with anyone. They had touched each other's essence.

He kissed along her jaw, moving to her lips, at first taking her lower lip and sucking gently on it and then moving to the top lip. Her mouth opened of its own accord and he was there, kissing deeply, his tongue caressing hers.

Grace moaned. Her blood sped around her body making parts of her throb. Declan held her round the back and his hands rose to cling to her shoulders, making her surrender further to his kisses. It was more than she'd imagined a date with him would be. All she'd had in the past was her imagination. His lips were so tender and the sensation they caused when they melded with hers made all restraint disappear. She kissed him back, licking along his lower lip, first smaller kisses and then lunging back in for a long drawn-out one that made her forget to breathe.

His fingers kneaded her scalp, chasing tension away. Her hands cupped his butt and those muscled mounds made her knees grow weak. He was all strength and hardness beneath his clothes.

Their kissing continued like a dance. They turned together in each other's arms, kissing necks and the tips of noses and then diving back in for the lips, for the mouth, tongues caressing. Declan's hands travelled down her sides and then reached around to cup her rear, pressing her body against his. That's when it got real.

Grace had to disentangle herself. She had to stop it right away. He couldn't know that she was untried.

He was obviously experienced. She would not have him laugh at her. Being a virgin right now was very inconvenient.

'Stop, please. I think we should leave it there. It's a mistake, really. We should just go home.'

'Why?' he said drowsily, his eyes heavy with arousal. He opened the circle of his arms, but he did not let her go free.

'We can't do this. We forget the situation.'

He pursed his lips. 'You like me, despite what you say. You can't hide the language of your body, your kisses. We could be great. We could be so close, if only…'

Grace closed her eyes. If only–the story of her life.

'There is no future for us, Declan Mallory. I ruined it ten years ago. Your parents would never accept me and I'm not interested in a one-night stand, a casual encounter.' She saw his eyes widen. She knew he didn't want a commitment. He'd told her so. She was on the right path now. She had to be firm.

'It could be fun.'

Grace shook ahead. She'd won this one. 'No. I'm afraid not.'

His arms dropped and he let her step away. She raced over to her shoes and slipped them on. 'Is there a train I can catch? You don't have to drive me home.'

'No, you're not catching a train.'

'Of course, I am.'

'Don't be ridiculous,' he said.

She bristled. '

Come on, Grace, there are two bedrooms, both made up. We can stay here. I won't touch you, if you don't want me to.'

Grace hesitated. Declan had backed off when she'd asked him to. He obviously wanted to stay in the cottage. It was lovely and she liked it too. 'Okay. Separate beds?'

'Only, if you insist.'

She narrowed her eyelids. 'Now, Declan Mallory, I'm not in the mood for games. What are you playing at?'

'Nothing, it's just it would be nice to hold you, Grace, to feel you close, even platonically. I really need that right now.'

Grace scoffed. 'What do you mean? You have so many girls after you.'

He waved a hand dismissively, and moved closer, speaking softly. 'They just want the prize. Can't you see how off-putting it is to be chased by all those witches? I'm lonely, Grace. I need to touch someone. I need you.'

Grace shook herself. 'Why me?'

He shrugged. 'I'm not entirely sure. We had a connection a long time ago. That draws me to you. Maybe it's because you know me and aren't chasing me. I can't explain it clearly to you.'

Grace blinked rapidly, trying to sort through her emotions and decipher Declan's reasoning. Grace couldn't let go of her skepticism. 'You want me but don't know why. That's not very flattering.'

'Grace, you accept me.'

'I do?'

He grinned and ruffled his hair. 'You don't worship me, or have an overblown idea of who I am. You're not interested in me as a catch, as a trophy. That's what those other witches want. I need the space you allow me to be me.'

She sensed that he was being honest. He really needed her and she couldn't walk away from that. There was more to this adult Declan than she'd first thought. He might seem as if he was reveling in all the attention, but in reality he wasn't. She wanted to ask more but didn't want to risk it. 'All right then. But play fair.'

Goddess, had she just agreed to sleep in the same bed as all that man? He'd better live up to his part of the deal, and no naughty business.

He leered at her. 'My honor as a warlock.'

Grace took her time in the shower as she contemplated what she had set herself up for. She was going to sleep in the same room as Declan, in the same bed. She'd only ever slept with Elena when they were young or snuggled with her mother when her mother was not otherwise occupied. She tried thinking back to when she was a girl; she'd never bunked up with Declan when they were kids. Their intimacy had been on a different level, mind-to-mind, and accidental, come to think of it. It had been so long since they had touched each other that way that is was less than a memory, more like the silk of a spider web touching her thoughts before dissolving completely.

The water ran cold and she hurriedly closed the taps. The hot water service wasn't an instantaneous system like she had at home. Hopefully, it recovered quickly or Declan was likely to be peeved with her for hogging all the hot water. As she dried herself, she eyed a pile of clothes he'd provided for her—a white singlet top and a pair of his boxer shorts. She brushed out her hair and absently used her talent to clean her own clothes and arrange them in a pile.

Grace used a touch of magic to dry her hair and style it neatly around her face and over her shoulders. She looked down at herself, dressed in the singlet shorts, and shrugged. Conjuring items was not one of her talents so she had little choice but to wear his clothes to bed. A neck-to-toe nightgown would have provided more comfort, perhaps with a padlock at the base to seal her in it. Despite his reassurance, she did feel that she was running the gauntlet in sleeping in the same bed with him. She brushed her lips with her fingers, remembering the heat of his kisses. Definitely taking risks there, as she had been seriously turned on.

Declan was leaning against the hallway wall when she opened the bathroom door. 'I'm sorry. I think I used all hot water.'

Declan laughed. 'That's fine. I'm quite set up for a cold shower.' He stepped into the bathroom, and Grace didn't know what to do with herself. Should she climb into bed and feign sleep or wait to be invited under the covers?

It had been a long day and she was rather done in. *Definitely in bed before him*, she thought. *And sound asleep*. That had to be her tactic.

There was a double bed in one room and a single in the other. She decided the double bed was the best option for sharing, particularly with such a large man. Her eyes rolled up *Goddess save me. I can't actually be doing this.*

Nerves aside, Grace rolled back the bedcovers and slid inside the clean-smelling sheets. Her handbag had been placed next to the bed. Declan must have moved it from the lounge room where she'd left it. Fetching her mobile phone, she quickly sent a text to Elena to let her know that she was fine, but gave no other details. She didn't want to be dealing with their questions and the potential for gossip. Elena returned a quick 'okay'.

Grace tossed the phone into her bag and lay back

against the pillows, staring at the ceiling. Fatigue mixed with wine caught up with her, making her eyelids heavy. She slid easily into sleep.

Her awareness returned when a muscled arm encircled her waist and drew her within the warmth of a large, firm body. Declan nuzzled at the back of her neck, his nose ruffling her hair. A sigh escaped her and she drifted back off to sleep. A warlock's honor? She'd never heard that they had any, but that thought drifted away.

Declan broadcast relaxing vibes as she nestled in the cradle of his arms. They tickled at her awareness, even in sleep. She wasn't sure if he did this on purpose or whether it was natural for him to do so. She was comforted rather than alarmed at being held so close, and basking in his warmth. His vibes made her experience comfort to her soul, such that she'd never thought she would feel ever again. Then her awareness sunk into unconsciousness.

Declan clung to Grace, luxuriating in the feel of her tight bottom snug against his groin. Her soft breathing was like a balm to his soul. Her trust and friendship were important to him. Until he returned to Sydney, he didn't know how much a part of him he'd left behind, and how much Grace filled up that empty space.

Moonlight filtered through the blinds, brightening the room and filling it with restless energy. Declan was not ready for sleep. He kissed Grace's shoulder, his mind filling with thoughts of her.

She demanded nothing from him and he liked that. The thought that it wasn't enough snuck up on him. He'd been avoiding entanglements, running from witches who were willing to give him anything he wanted. Except for Grace. She wanted nothing from him.

Begrudgingly, she'd offered friendship.

If he wanted more from her, he was going to have to demand it. She was too wounded to freely give to him. It wasn't just the betrayal that day when they were kids. There had been years of suffering at the hands of others. It didn't take him long to get the full story of how she'd been treated during his time away. The slights he'd witnessed recently were only mild in comparison to her school years. Her family had supported her, and that was all. Her family was her center, and he understood that. But was it enough? Was it a full life?

There was too much angst and stormy waters churning through broken bridges for her to be open with him. She'd said as much when he'd asked her to touch his mind like she had when she was a child. He could mind speak her, but he couldn't reach out and touch like she had the power to do.

He did not tell her about his own family's animosity towards the Denholm clan, and he couldn't think of a way to shift it. Not right then. They didn't know he was with Grace now, in this house. He made sure to keep the boundaries of his life tight, and as much as he loved his family, he wasn't about to tell them every single thing that he did or reveal who he was intimate with. There was time enough to deal with that when he'd decided to settle down.

He'd learned a lot about Grace; enough to know that she had an amazing courage that stood against what the members of the coven had thrown at her. She was a bit of a prodigy with her talent, able to touch people's essences, their souls. That was why she'd been able to summon the spirit of her cat all those years ago. At that time, she hadn't understood the boundaries between life and death. Now, she was so controlled she wasn't using her talent at all. That was a damn shame. Yes, necromancy was strongly associated with dark magic, forbidden magic, but there had to be ways to use her ability for good.

The subsequent tutoring from the elders had not only enhanced her skills, but taught her to navigate between life and death so that she couldn't commit that awful sin of bringing back the dead again. Yet her talent gave her many advantages, such as being able to understand people, find hidden spells and dark motivations. He grinned, thinking of their match that afternoon. She was strong in mental agility too. She easily matched his own. She'd make a strong warrior if she chose. He considered her spirit, so light and airy after a lifetime of shame and ostracism. It had taken her a lot of inner strength to turn out as well she did, given the circumstances. He could only admire her.

Holding her close tested his vow not to make love to her. He sensed that she was dreaming and he was sorely tempted to take a peek inside. He'd could only skim the surface, not touch her essence. He remembered when she had reached out to him, and in their innocence they had shared parts of themselves. Was that a fluke? Could they do such a thing again? It was so long ago.

Grace changed positions but Declan wasn't ready to turn away from her, so he maneuvered her so that she lay along his body, her face on his shoulder, her arm across his middle. Her knee rested on his. He lay there with Grace in his arms, staring at the ceiling and trying not to think about his arousal.

Grace's consciousness rose up from her dream.

She was in that in-between space where being not quite aware, she would answer questions if asked.

'Grace?'

'Mmm.'

'You're a virgin, aren't you?' he whispered in her ear. She mumbled something incomprehensible but he knew that was it. What else could she be? Unless she'd taken up with humans, she was bound to be untouched. There weren't that many warlocks in the coven and she had been shunned. No one would date her for fear of her necromancy.

The kisses they had shared that night were more than special, knowing that he was probably the only one. Yet it also worried him because Grace had passion inside of her. She did a good job of keeping it banked to a low ember. The desire to unleash it solidified.

He wasn't about to break his word, but he was going to mine heavily along the edges.

Reaching across her body with his free hand, he stroked along her jaw. He passed his thumb over her bottom lip, smiling when she tried to dislodge it as though he were a fly buzzing around her head. Gently, he eased her face upwards and pressed his lips against hers. He sent a mental thrust of encouragement. *Come on, Grace. Kiss me.*

Grace was waking up. She opened her mouth and accepted his tongue, which was so ready to rub against hers. Her hand slid from his waist to his neck, while his slid along her back to cup her butt. With a quick maneuver, she was lying across him, giving his hands free access to knead her bottom. As she responded, he enjoyed the feel of her *mons* grinding against his erection. He'd said he wouldn't do this but she wasn't exactly protesting.

His hands slid inside her boxer shorts, reveling in

the feel of her warm, firm flesh in his hands. Grace squirmed, inadvertently rubbing herself harder against him. His eyes rolled up, a groan sounding low in his throat. She was going to kill him.

He broke off the kiss and moved her to his side. His mouth dived straight to a nipple revealed through the oversized singlet she was wearing. Grace's body stiffened and an impassioned cry escaped from her throat. The sound made him even harder. He could picture himself sliding inside her, catching her cries of ecstasy in his mouth. He switched to the other nipple. Grace surrendered herself to him, thrusting her breast so that he could reach it easily.

'Don't stop,' she mumbled.

His fingers slid into her moist folds and found her clitoris. Grace cried out in a loud voice as he stroked. She was a witch, who was at one with the goddess. He could sense the sexual energy surging within her.

Oh, how he wanted to sink inside of her, but he couldn't. He leaned his head against hers and panted. She was a virgin and it was wrong to take her like this. He'd touched a nerve and she was ready, aching with need. Vulnerable.

It had to be her choice. A rational choice, not one made in a moment of passion like this. He may not be able to seek satisfaction between her legs but he could certainly provide her first taste.

Flipping her on to her back, Declan tugged her boxer shorts lower and he kissed down her center-line, nibbling on her tight belly before burying his face in her sweet sex. She cried out again as he gently suckled, stroking her clitoris with his tongue in a rhythm that soon had her writhing and then screaming while she tugged on his hair. He held her by the hips, pleasuring her, giving her what he hoped was her first orgasm.

Her body was possessed by jerks and twitches as pleasure rippled through her. He was gratified that he had done that, brought her to climax. He climbed up her body, holding her close, as she lay languid in his arms.

It wasn't right that such intimacy had been denied her. He'd had plenty of encounters as he grew up. Warlocks had to be able to pleasure their witches if they wanted to keep them. How sad that Grace had to wait until she was twenty-two. No wonder she was angry with him. No wonder she hadn't wanted anything to do with him. He thought himself a jerk for taking their platonic sleepover to another level, but he couldn't regret making her cry out like that, hearing that special sound coming from her lips. He had been well-intentioned. They had shared a touching of the minds as a child, an event that was now a distant memory that had been replaced by this one. He would treasure it always—nurture it, because he never wanted to forget what he'd been able to give her.

Grace still throbbed from her amazing orgasm. Where had her resolve gone? Probably with those racy dreams she was having before he woke her and chased them away. Sleeping with a platonic Declan was obviously not a good idea, unless one wanted to be driven crazy with lust. Perhaps she should have been the one to have a cold shower. She sighed. He held her so tenderly she wanted to weep.

'Grace?'

'Mmm.' She didn't want to talk. She wanted more of where that came from.

'Grace?' He nudged her.

She lifted herself up and rested on her side with her hand supporting her head. As she looked up into his face, shrouded in shadows, she let out a long sigh. *Goddess above and below. She was in bed with a gorgeous hunk of a man.* Who'd have thought skinny Declan Mallory would fill out so well? His father was short and sort of dumpy, so you wouldn't have supposed it.

'Is my honor still intact?'

'What honor? You're a warlock and a trickster.'

He pursed his lips.

Grace laughed. 'Don't worry. I could have shut you down if I wanted to.'

His eyebrows rose, a look of skepticism.

'Look, I think we've gone past recriminations and well into explorations now. You've been exploring my anatomy so I think it's only fair I investigate yours. I seem to recall a rather large bulge.'

A cross between a squeak and a laugh escaped him. 'Now, Grace. You're a virgin. I don't want to—'

'Oh damn.' She sat up. 'I'm an inconvenient virgin. That truly sucks.'

His fingers brushed the side of her face. 'Not inconvenient, but you should save it for someone special. After all, you've waited this long, what's another few days...months...'

'Years.'

'That's a bit pessimistic.'

'Is it? Oh goddess, you should live my life.'

'Look, it's not even about whether you're a virgin or not. I'm not ready to settle down. I've got things I want to do. I wouldn't want to give rise to expectations. I'm not the one you should share your first time with.'

'Oh, give over all ready.'

'I'm glad I gave you your first orgasm.'

Grace sat up in bed. 'Are you kidding me? I've had plenty of those.'

'Oh, yes. I suppose you pleasure yourself. How arrogant of me.'

'Damn straight you're arrogant. Madam Eloise ran me through the paces when I turned eighteen. Mother insisted, as she didn't want me growing up to be a shriveled up old prude. Besides, the goddess encourages us to explore our sexuality.'

'Madam Eloise, the French witch from Nice? She was my first,' he admitted.

'Taught you all the tricks then,' Grace quipped. 'Excellent.' Her hands dived to the sheet covering him. 'So let's check out this enormous and possibly painful erection of yours.'

He grabbed the sheet and covered himself. 'Now Grace. We should talk about this.'

Grace flicked on the lamp, using her power to make it a low glow. She was really interested in seeing his equipment. She straddled his thighs and put her hands on her hips. 'Come on then. Either we employ your equipment or you take me home right now to Randy Roger.'

'Who?'

'Randy Roger.'

'Who's that?' His forehead creased.

'My vibrator. It's only small but it does the job.'

He laughed so hard he nearly knocked her off her perch. Then their eyes met and passion burned in his. Her senses slid inside for a second and she nearly choked. This was a hot man, a sensual man, and she was directly in his sights.

He sighed. 'Of course you use a vibrator. Madam Eloise's first lesson. Learn your own body, learn to pleasure yourself and you can give to others as well as to yourself.'

'Yes. I have my self-pleasuring down to an art.'

'Show me.'

Grace rocked back. *So much for teasing. Can't stop now.* 'On one condition. I get to check out that throbbing cock of yours.'

'You betch ya.'

Grace stripped off her singlet. She'd lost her boxers earlier when Declan had been using his tongue so expertly. She got on all fours, butt angled in the air. She put a finger on her clitoris and stroked. Declan appeared to choke.

Then she thought she'd mind share her erotica image, the one that always brought her to climax. It was rather ribald. 'Then there's this.'

Declan sat up, smacked her lightly on the butt. She turned around, kneeling on the bed, facing him. 'You want me to take you up the ass?' he asked, titillated by the image she'd shared.

'Declan.' She sighed. 'It's a fantasy. Not real. It's just an image, a scene that resonates with me. It's very personal.'

Grace jerked her head in the direction of his erection. 'Show time.'

Declan laid back against the pillow and slowly lowered the sheet. 'Oh, by the goddess!' Grace covered her mouth, then shook her head. 'You're definitely not doing me up the ass with that. It's enormous.'

'I've had my share of compliments.'

'I'll bet.' She leaned in close to look at it, comparing it from different angles. She had serious doubts it would fit in any woman's vagina, particularly hers. Yet he'd pleasured her and she wanted to return the favor. She'd never had a real flesh cock in her mouth before. Madam Eloise's dildo was realistic but not real.

'I think we should try stripping the bark.'

His head jerked up off the pillow. 'What?'

Grace shrugged. 'I'll show you. Much easier than explaining.'

Grace attacked the side of his penis, lathing up the sides and then sucking on the way down. Declan nearly dislodged her. Perhaps Madam Eloise had not demonstrated that one to the warlocks. She did that for a few minutes, liking how his breath was ragged. 'Now, I think we should try the vortex.'

'Vortex?' His voice was a harsh whisper.

Her tongue slid around the edge of the tip, going faster until she had him full in the mouth. She had to hold his erection still because he was shoving his hips up and pounding the mattress with his fists. Her senses drifted over to him, catching the images and erotic thoughts passing through his mind. She joined with them. He thought her erotic images were odd. In his mind, she drank a tank-load of him. Not quite physically possible, she was sure.

She rose up off him and licked her lips. 'So what's it to be? My way or the highway?'

He nodded but didn't move. It looked like she'd have to take the initiative. When she climbed up and suspended herself above him, she did think it was going to be impossible. Her hips were small. She was rather slightly built. Rubbing his head against herself, she lined him up, ready to sink onto him. She didn't get very far. Declan was shaking, the restraint killing him.

He was only in a short way and then she stopped. His hands grabbed her around the hips and he lifted her and then urged her down. He went a little further in. It was taking a long time. No heavy-hipped thrust, this was a gradual penetration. It didn't hurt. It wasn't that. It was a size thing. He groaned as she slid down him again, sinking a little further. The sound he made encouraged her slickness. It was working. They were getting into a rhythm.

She rose up and then lowered again. Looking down, she wondered how she would accommodate his length as he wasn't all in. Once again he raised her up and then brought her down, his strength working with her weight until she was fully impaled.

Tremors overtook her. He was inside her. She couldn't move. Staked, she was. Stretched. Full.

'I can't move,' she whispered, a tad embarrassed.

Declan moved under her, an upthrust that had her looking for something to hold onto. She slid back down him and groaned. That was a spot Randy Roger never hit. He did it again and she cried out. A climax built quickly. She was losing herself to the sensation of him moving and thrusting inside her. Soon she was liquid. Declan disengaged from her and she felt so empty. He rearranged her on the bed, had her on all fours. She had to lower herself so that he could enter her. His strong hands on her hips gave her heart-thudding pleasure. His cock stroked her until she was screaming into the sheets, gripping them in her hands. She was spread so wide she couldn't move except for where he guided her. Who would have thought a vagina could provide such pleasure?

Her senses roamed out again, seeking to touch what was leaking from his mind. He was so in the moment. His cock was the focus of intense stimulation, the feel of her buttocks hitting the tops of his thighs like clouds of lust, her dark slit a moist heaven where he could play. Those thoughts merged with her own. He came suddenly with a roar. Her scream was not only in her mind. As they flopped on the bed, she swore she could hear the echoes of their pleasure still bouncing in the rafters.

'Oh, Grace.'

'My thoughts exactly, Declan Mallory.'

She dimmed the light completely and they drifted off to sleep, entwined in each other.

CHAPTER FOUR

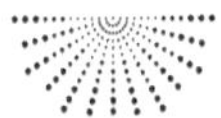

Grace was dreaming. A rather gorgeous hunk of a man was licking her clitoris with an expert tongue. The light brightened and she became aware of the room, aware of Declan pleasuring her between her legs.

'Oh goddess!' was all she could manage before she climaxed. That was unexpected. She'd gone from the occasional romp with her little mechanical man to having three, or was it four close encounters of the sexual kind in a twelve-hour period.

'Good morning,' Declan said, plonking his head between her breasts. 'I love to hear your heart beat like that. You make mine beat double-time.'

She ran her fingers through his hair, liking the silken feel of it. 'You're welcome. If word gets out you wake your sex partners up with oral sex, the stalking will increase ten-fold.'

He lifted his head and met her gaze, his expression serious. 'You won't tell.'

Grace shook her head. 'No way. Our secret.'

'Come on then. I'll buy you breakfast on the road. I best get back home.'

'So your parents don't know you're here.'

He rolled off the bed, easing both his shoulders. 'No. I said I was going out for a while.'

'Is everything okay at home?'

'Sure. It's just I'm a man, and I like to have some privacy. I think you know how intrusive families can be, and the coven too, if you don't put up boundaries.'

Grace nodded. 'Sure, but I'm used to it. We are very close, my mother and Elena and I.'

'Elvira Denholm is known for her tolerance, unlike my…'

Grace stood up and cringed slightly. So lovemaking did leave traces. She quickly healed the slight tear in her tender flesh and took another step. Nothing more than stretched muscles and lack of sleep to blame for the rest. 'Mother is a firm follower of the goddess. Sex is very important to her.'

'But your father is gone, isn't he?'

Grace searched the floor for her singlet and boxers. Best to give them back to Declan.

'My father is in New Orleans at the moment. He's met a powerful witch over there and she's expecting a daughter. I'll have a half-sister.'

'So your mother finds other men to satisfy her needs?'

'Pretty much. Although she is pretty discreet about it. She likes her privacy too, although she tells us everything.'

Grace found her clothes and climbed into them. Declan must think her family was weird. His parents had stayed together. She gave a mental shrug. Some chose to do that, particularly when there was love involved. Ernst and Elvira hadn't loved one another. Not in the way that mattered. It was a pairing to produce a child. They had an arrangement and that ended by mutual agreement.

Declan left the room and went to the bathroom. Grace spelled the sheets clean and made the bed, while checking they had left nothing behind. She also killed any sperm. Declan had been pretty clear he wanted no entanglements.

After her turn in the bathroom, Declan cleared the house of any rubbish. It was like they hadn't even been there, except for the sounds of their lovemaking soaking into the wood.

Back on the bike, Grace marveled at how different it felt when she put her arms around him. When she touched him, ripples of pleasure sped through her skin. Closing her eyes, she rested her face on his back, liking the solid feel of him. They had shared something special the previous night. She'd been able to be herself with him, and he was not repulsed by her. She'd met his demand for intimacy with her own and he'd fronted up to that, no quibbles. The heat of his thoughts sent sizzles into her brain. Those were only leaked. What if they had met mind to mind? Was it even safe to do that? Nowhere to hide. No way to block. She had best not try it.

Unlike the trip up to the mountains, the trip back passed quickly. Declan dropped her back to her car at the school.

He parked the bike and drew her close, kissing the top of her head. 'Thank you, Grace. That was an amazing experience.'

She hugged him. 'Any time you want a platonic bed mate, check me out.' She meant it.

He nodded and backed away, his hazel-brown eyes melting her to the core. *Oh dear, I've got it bad. That's no good.*

With her butt leaning on her bonnet, she watched him drive away. Blowing air to dislodge her fringe, she shook her head. There were no regrets. She was glad she'd finally been laid and over the moon it had been with Declan. So he didn't want a commitment— at least she didn't feel unworthy as she had at first, when all those gorgeous bitch-witches had been chasing him down. It was their secret but she could hold her head high.

When she had gathered her wits, she slipped behind the wheel of her car and went home. Elena was sprawled on the couch and her mother was in the garden, sending good vibes to her basil, which was seriously threatening to die on her.

'Grace? You're back,' Elena said, pushing hair drowsily out of her eyes.

Grace sniffed. 'Obviously. Hey, move over. I need to snuggle.'

Elena made room for her, targeting her with her gaze. 'Where have you been? Wait, something is different. Oh my god, you've been laid.' Elena bounced around on the couch. 'Grace has been laid. Grace has been laid,' she shouted, her exuberance making Grace smile.

'Easy. Quiet. Mother will hear you.'

Elvira walked in and plonked a sad-looking bunch of herbs on the bench. 'Where have you been, young lady?' She did a double take. 'Who was it?'

Grace cradled a cushion against her chest and pretended to be absorbed in the sitcom Elena had blaring on the television.

The screen went blank. Elvira had killed it. 'Speak, child.'

'I'm not a child.' Heat radiated from her cheeks. 'It's private.'

She looked to Elena for support. 'No,' her cousin scoffed. 'What makes you think that anything is private in this family?' Then she laughed at Grace's shocked expression. 'Come on, Grace, spill. You dragged the story of my first time out of me. Fair is fair.'

Elvira pulled out a stool and dragged it into the lounge room. 'You were seen on a motorbike with Declan Mallory.'

Grace rolled her eyes at the ceiling. 'Goddess. Is nothing sacred?'

'There is a story circulating that he kissed you in front of the school.'

Grace coughed into her hand and colored up.

Elena turned to Elvira. 'She got laid.'

Elvira looked smug. 'I can see that myself.' She sat there thinking for a minute. 'Was it Declan Mallory?'

Her guess was spot on. Grace had the grace to blush even more.

'Tell us all about it,' Elena said sitting up straighter.

'No. I'm not. It's our secret.'

Elena and Elvira burst out laughing. 'You're crazy to think that, Gracie,' Elena said

'Dearest. We know who and we know what. All we want is the details.' Both Elvira and Elena laughed even harder. Grace chewed her cheek, not sure whether to laugh with them or smack their bottoms.

Elvira staggered to her feet, still laughing uproariously, and went to the fridge. Three champagne flutes appeared on the coffee table. 'This calls for a celebration,' Elvira said from the open fridge. 'I have some Bollinger here I was saving for a special occasion.

'But it's too early to drink.' Grace folded her arms, and pouted. It had been her secret for about five minutes.

'Who says?' Elena asked and then nudged her.

Elvira brought the wine over and popped it open, making the cork materialize in Grace's lap. 'Oh?'

Elvira poured them a drink each. Grace took a long draft of hers.

For the rest of the afternoon and into the evening, they sat there listening raptly as Grace gave them a blow-by-blow account of her first sexual encounter with a real, flesh man. They were on the second bottle and rolling on the floor laughing by the time she'd finished. They loved her description of being impaled on Declan and not being able to move.

'Classic,' Elena said.

Elvira wiped her eyes. 'I'm glad you had a good first time, my darling girl. It makes so much difference to your life. Declan is a good man. A good choice.'

Grace's smile dropped. 'Ah, don't get ideas, Mother. It was strictly a one-night, no-commitment thing.'

Elvira stood up on unsteady legs. 'He'll be back. Mark my words.' She lurched a bit. 'One taste of a Denholm witch and he's a lost warlock.'

She stood straighter, holding the back of the chair. Her hand went to her forehead. 'Oh, that's not good.' She laid her gaze on them and then nodded. 'I best take myself off. Good night.'

Grace watched as her mother wobbled down the hall to her bedroom. She glanced at Elena, who was covering a large yawn with her hand. 'I might go to bed too.'

'Right. I'll just pop off to bed then too. I'll shower first.'

Declan parked his bike and chained it to the carport. He sent a mental hello to his parents, and, with a sigh, detected their relief. He'd stayed away the rest of the day after dropping Grace home. They were not adjusting well to his need to have a private life. It was like they wanted to live their lives vicariously through his. As much as he loved and cared for them, he wasn't up for that. He was grateful to them for being the loving and caring parents that they were. He was thankful for their support and for their unflinching pride in all his achievements. But he needed and wanted to live his own life and make his own choices. He was not going to settle down with a witch of their choice and produce grandchildren at their behest. Negotiating this position was the hardest thing he'd ever had to do.

When he opened the front door both his parents appeared at the end of the hallway, their expressions full of worry. A stab of guilt punctured him deep in the gut. Definitely the hardest thing he'd ever done.

'Hello. How are you both?' he asked as he sauntered down the hall to the kitchen. He gave his mother a peck on her cheek and she lifted tear-stained eyes in his direction. 'Dad?'

'You were gone all night. We were worried.'

'I told you I'd be out and not to worry.'

'But we do worry. Please don't do that again.'

Declan scanned the clean kitchen, the place setting still there for himself. 'I can't promise you that I won't go out again without telling you specifically where I'll be. Come on, Dad. I need space, freedom.

'You have a duty to the coven, to us. Don't you respect that? Have you so little—'

'Dad. It's got nothing to do with duty or love. It's

about respecting me as an adult, letting me make my own decisions.'

'Like being with that woman?'

Declan stilled. 'What woman?'

'You were seen with that Riordon woman.'

'Her name is Grace, Dad. You know that. She and I were close when we were young.'

'I know who and what she is. I forbid you to see her again. She will never be welcome here in this family.'

Declan threw his head back and laughed. 'Don't worry about that. I'm not going to settle down with anyone. If you listened to me, you'd know that. I don't want to settle down. I want to make my own way, make my own choices.'

'Declan. You can't mean that,' his mother said in her soft tones. 'The coven needs children. You must procreate.'

'I can do that without settling down if I must, but I won't. I wouldn't abandon a child of mine.'

Declan's father rubbed his forehead. 'Please, son, listen to your mother. I don't care who you father a child with, but stay away from that woman. She's trouble. Her family is trouble.'

Declan stood up, squeezing his fists together. 'Dad, I said leave it alone. Grace is a beautiful person, full of light and love. She doesn't deserve any of this mud you fling her way or the bad treatment meted out by the rest of the coven. She's a powerful witch, too. You should see her—'

'I don't need to. I've seen enough from her family.'

Declan walked forward, and his father and mother had to step back to give him room. 'I'm going to bed.' He turned away and then paused. 'No. Wait,' he said, facing them. 'I want you to tell me what it is about Grace's family that's got you so uptight.'

His parents shared a look. His mother tilted her head as if to say go ahead.

'Alright. Declan, please. Sit down,' his father said

Suppressing a groan, Declan tugged out a chair at the kitchen table and took a seat. His parents sat either side of him. His mother took his hand and squeezed it. He returned the pressure.

'You know Elvira's sister, the one who caused a few "issues" before she left?'

Declan shrugged. 'Yes, I've heard the rumors.'

'Well, what is not widely known is that Elvira had a brother. A younger brother.'

Declan sat back, surprised. 'I haven't heard of him.'

'Elroy. He—'

Declan's gaze switched between his parents. His mother chewed her bottom lip and she sniffed loudly. 'He killed my brother,' she said in a voice so quiet Declan thought he'd heard it wrong.

'He did more than that. He killed a number of warlocks,' his father added. 'One was my cousin.'

'How come people don't talk about this? I don't get it, and I still don't get what this has got to do with Grace. She hasn't killed anyone. She has the opposite problem.'

'This is no joke, son. For years after, witches selectively stopped giving birth to males. That's why there is a shortage of warlocks. It wasn't planned, it just happened.'

'It was an instinctive reaction,' his mother added, watching him closely. 'I didn't abide by it myself.'

'Elroy Denholm was ten years old, Declan. Samuel was four.'

A leaden feeling grew in his gut. 'How many other boys did he kill before he was stopped?'

'Three,' his mother said.

'Three warlocks. We don't know how many humans he might have killed.' His father slapped his hand down on the table.

'Grace doesn't know this, does she?'

His mother's eyes narrowed. 'Who cares if she does or not? The whole family is tainted.'

Declan sat back, astounded. 'No, they aren't. What if I did something wrong? Would you like to be tarred with the same brush, shunned and blamed for something you didn't do? You raised me the best you could but I'm responsible for my own life, my own decisions.

'Goddess. That's it. That's why you are clinging so hard, trying to direct me, control my life. You don't want me to do anything that shames you, anything that deviates from your view of the world. You're worried what the coven would say, what other people think.'

'No, son.' His father reached up, grabbed him by the shoulder. 'That's not true. You could never shame us.'

His mother wiped her eyes. 'No. You are my pride and my heart. Nothing you could do to change that but...we want you to stay away from Grace Riordon. There are plenty of other witches to choose from. I don't understand why you would even think of her.'

Declan stood up, shaking with helpless rage. 'Because it's my choice, Mother. I sleep with a woman or the women I choose. Not one chosen for me or thrust in my way.'

'Yes, but you must make sure you have all the facts,' added his mother. 'You cannot mix your seed with that family. I won't have it.' She started heaving in large breaths, her face going pale. His father leaned over and rubbed her back. 'It's all right, Del. Relax.'

To Declan he said, 'We are just trying to understand you, guide you.'

'Really? Then stay out of my life choices. If I ask for advice feel free to give it, but don't ever comment about Grace or any other woman I take to my bed.'

His mother gasped, covering her mouth with her hand.

'You slept with Grace Riordon?' His father gaped at him.

Declan was beyond angry now. He had a lot to process. 'Yes, and I was her first. Her first lover at twenty-two because this coven has isolated her so much no decent warlock will go near her. That's what your hate and distrust have done.'

'It's not as simple as that. You forget what happened before we left, why we left.'

'I've not forgotten anything. I was there, remember? What she did was an innocent mistake. It wasn't evil. I wish you'd damn well get that. Grace has the lightest and loveliest spirit of anyone I have ever met. She's no dark witch.'

His mother began to cry, but Declan was over it. He'd comforted his mother often when she'd cried, done what she'd asked so as not to upset her. It was time he hardened up. He turned away.

The bloody coven with their secrets and rules had him fuming. They'd made a mess of everything and then left the younger generation to deal with it. Well, he'd had enough of that. He stomped down the hall and took a long shower. Later, as he tried to sleep, he couldn't. He needed a balm for the hurt inside; he needed something soft and gentle to soothe his mind. He needed Grace.

By the time Grace was ready for bed it was near three a.m. She looked around the room at her wall of crazy hats and the quilt that she and Elena had sewn in their first year together, and wondered if this was what her life was going to be—this room, this house, this sense of being unfulfilled.

Admittedly, losing her virginity to Declan Mallory was bit of an achievement. She couldn't say that he had not fulfilled her as the tenderness was a tangible reminder. She sent some more healing there, even though it was kind of a cool reminder of their hot encounter. She chuckled to herself, recollecting her mother's joy and Elena's incredulity as she had related and embellished her first sexual encounter. As she flipped back the quilt and climbed between the sheets, she sensed her world was on a precipice— that she was going to fall and fall hard, or she was going to take off with wings into the sky and float and glide to a glorious future.

'You're being ridiculous. He said it was a one-night thing. You have to respect that.' She huddled into the pillow and stared at the wall, her eyes trailing from the picture of her father to the one with her and Elena with Declan in the background, from when they were young. She struggled to find that thirteen-year-old girl inside of her as she studied the innocent faces, her dark eyes and her bright smile.

Her focus shifted to Declan, looking at the child and comparing it to his adult face. His eyes were still dark in his high-cheekboned face and his smile, too, was reminiscent of the boy she had known. Yet he was tall and broad and a man now. His life experiences had shaped him, had changed him. One thing, though, was the same—the essence of him—he was still that Declan, and if that was the case, she was still that Grace, even though she had been through so much, had borne so much from others. How could that be?

She'd survived years of being shunned, of being ignored and overlooked, and in some cases despised. It was because she had love—the love of her mother and father. She had a very close bond with Elena.

Other than that, Grace had love for the world, had love for herself and for the goddess who lived in all things. That was her anchor, her true protection. She had been born with talents and her parents had encouraged her to explore them. She had an affinity with spirit. She could sense people; she could sense illness, evil and spells that affected them. Although she was not free to use this power whenever she chose; she had to seek permission, or be requested. That was how she'd spent the last nine years—learning, being drilled, so that her talent was bounded by the rules.

The clock displayed 4.30 a.m. She was exhausted and yet her mind was still alive with feelings and ideas. Yet, she had to lie there and try to sleep because her family would not appreciate it if she got up and started moving around.

Grace sat up suddenly. A ripple in the house ward sent shards of electricity over her skin. Then there was a sound outside her window; someone was there. One of the coven who was allowed to pass through her mother's wards. She was about to send her senses out to find out who when there was a tap at her window. Grace flung off the quilt and padded over. A shadow loomed and then resolved into the familiar face of Declan. She undid the latch on the window and opened it out.

'Is something wrong? Is everything all right?'

'Everything is fine. I just wanted to spend some time with you.'

'With me? Right here, right now?'

She caught the outline of his shrug. Momentarily speechless, she could only step back from the window and nod. It was probably not the right time to quibble about the 'one night' thing. Obviously, he was upset about something.

He climbed in through the window, knocking a few hats off the wall. Grace repositioned them without taking her eyes off him. He was in the bike leathers. They made him so much bigger, broader, and hot as all hell. His dark brows knitted together.

'What is it?' she asked.

'Stuff,' he said with a grunt.

'Okay. So you didn't come here to talk.' She stepped back to give him room.

'No,' he said with a growl, and drew her to him. He nuzzled her neck and she went all weak and floaty, edging up on her toes for more and reveling in his delicious bite. The switch had flipped and her clitoris was throbbing like a beacon within a minute. Who needed talk?

His lips brushed across hers, and she moaned at the excruciating, teasing friction. She didn't want gentle and restrained. She wanted hot, demanding and all-encompassing passion. She caught his soft bottom lip between her teeth and tugged gently. Declan growled louder and she released it.

'You must be tender,' he whispered in her ear. 'I thought we should go slowly.'

'Slowly? We still have our clothes on. Nothing fast about that. Besides, I fixed myself. I feel fine.'

He chuckled and held her face between his palms, gazing into her eyes. 'You're amazing, you know that?

Cheeky too. You should respect me more. I'm a battle master.'

'Ha.' She kissed the end of his nose. 'You're a puppy. A big, sweet—'

Being unceremoniously tossed on the bed cut her off. Declan had his jacket off, and his boots were undoing themselves as he approached.

'Eep,' she said, edging further up the bed. His eyes glittered and he had a devilish grin on his face, the sight of which made her belly turn over and her toes tingle. He stopped at the edge of the bed, undoing the buckle on his leather pants.

'Take off your clothes,' he said gruffly.

Raising herself up on her elbows, she replied, 'Make me.'

His pants were gone, his boxers soon after. Before she could draw breath, she had six-foot four of large male covering her and a rather convincing erection nestled between her thighs. 'Now, you were saying?'

'Make me?' She was less cheeky and more awed.

He lifted himself up on all fours, her lying between his legs. She was wearing an old pajama set, shorts with a top. 'These a favorite of yours?'

She shook her head, her heart somewhere between her breast and her throat. The buttons pinged as they ricocheted off the walls. He moved down her body and grabbed her shorts with his teeth and ripped, leaving her naked. Grace nearly fainted with desire. What a turn on. With a growl, he lunged his tongue between her labia with rapid strokes that had her arching her back before she could draw breath.

'Goddess!' she cried out, so close to coming, she didn't need her erotic mind picture. She was in the moment, feeling every stroke of his tongue. Her hands gripped the bed covers and her breaths were loud. Whimpers leaked out of her mouth and then the moment came and she couldn't stop the yell as she cried out in ecstasy.

Declan's mouth sought hers. Grace was mush. She surrendered. She kissed him; she sent her tongue so deep she thought she might swallow him whole.

A mental query came from her mother. ????

Grace couldn't even engage. Her mind was full of Declan, Declan, Declan.

She sensed the amusement from her mother. Elena knocked on the bedroom door. 'Grace. Are you okay?'

She clung to Declan's naked chest, panting. After swallowing to give her time to find her breath, she called out, 'It's okay. Just with Declan. Sorry.'

'Okay.' Elena walked away.

Declan chuckled. 'So much for secrecy and sneaking around. You woke the neighborhood.'

She slapped his chest lightly, then turned it into a caress. 'It's your fault. You made me come so loud. Next time give me warning when you leap from the shadows. I could have mentally prepared myself for the onslaught.'

He laughed then and flipped her onto her back. 'Not on your life. I love how you are so open, so real. Don't change it.' She lifted her hands, palms up, and he rested his against them. 'This thing we have is amazing, addictive.'

Grace nodded. 'What are you waiting for? I believe Randy Roger is getting twitchy in my bedside drawer.'

With a growl that thrilled her to the spine, Declan angled himself for a quick entry. 'I'm afraid Randy Roger might never do the job again,' Declan observed.

'Promises, promises.'

He slid slowly inside her, holding her hips in his

hands and angling to maximize the ease of entry. Grace was yelling again, not quite aware of how loudly. It was all blood-pumping, heart-thudding and soul-stroking awesomeness. This man could fuck. *Oh goddess.*

The initial thrusts had her climaxing again, but Declan wasn't done. He rode her hard. The old bed-head banged against the walls. Grace reached up and clung to it while being pummeled so delightfully.

Sweat beaded on his skin. Grace let go the bed-head and ran a hand along his smooth chest, leaning up to lick his saltiness. Declan nearly lost a hold of her. She ran her thumb over his right breast and licked it too, stopping to suckle a hard nipple. Declan cried out, and with a roar, held her hips tight while he ground himself against her. He folded himself over her carefully, leaving a trail of kisses along her neck and capturing her mouth for a soul-wrenching kiss that sent her spirit spiraling to the heavens.

Wow! This sex thing is really awesome. Much better than self-pleasure, no matter what they say.

'I'm glad you think so.'

Grace stilled. 'You heard that?'

'Yes, clear as a bell.'

'But I didn't say anything. I thought it.'

He blinked at her, uncomprehendingly at first, then the light dawned in his eyes. 'We're connected.'

'A little,' she said, frowning. 'I didn't mean to project to you. I didn't mean to breach your boundaries.'

'No, no, don't. It was a lovely moment. Please don't try to apologize. I was open. You were open. It just happened. No need for apologies.'

Grace relaxed, relieved that she hadn't transgressed.

Grey light outside flowed in through the open

window. Dawn was not far away. 'Now, do you want to talk about it?'

Declan lay back and gathered Grace into his arms. His forehead rested against hers. 'Not really. I had a "discussion" with my parents.'

'About me?'

'Sort of, but it was more than that. Do you remember your uncle, Elroy?'

'No. I have an Uncle Elroy?'

'Had, apparently.'

Grace chewed her lip. 'That's odd. I mean, mother has not spoken of him. Why, did he do something bad?'

Declan stroked the hair from her shoulder. 'It's not good; not a nice story. It's best you ask your mother.'

'I will when she wakes up.' She refrained from mentally signaling her mother right then. Declan was still opening up. She couldn't get distracted now.

'And...'

Declan sighed. 'Look, it's not a biggy. It's me trying to get some space between me and my parents. They've got my life laid out for me. I want to choose my own path. I can't seem to reason with them. They come up with all these reasons why I must do my duty, follow their direction and I can't abide it. I love them. I don't want to hurt them, but the need in me to be free of their restraint is too powerful.'

She reached up and stroked his hair out of his eyes. 'It must be difficult.' There was a noise at the window. The ghostly outline of Fel, the cat, pranced along the sill.

'That's her, isn't it? Elena's cat.'

'Yes, Fel.'

He shook his head. 'What an amazing thing. You don't do anything to sustain it?'

'No. I don't do anything. It has a life of its own. Mother thinks the cat had supernatural ability before I…you know…helped it. It talks, you know. Sends little snarky barbs into your brain.'

He looked askance at her. 'No. You're joking me, right?'

'I am not, Declan Mallory. I would not joke about something like that.'

Fel purred. He's grown into a big tom.

'See? She just said you've grown into a big tom. She's not wrong there.'

'I didn't hear anything.' His eyes were wide, eyebrows raised.

'I'm not lying.' Grace tried to get off the bed, suddenly miffed at his incredulous look, but he brought her back easily. 'Let me go, you big oaf.'

'Don't be angry with me, Grace. It's just a cat.'

'That's the problem, isn't it? It's not just a cat.' Her face was screwed up with anger. She wanted to punch him.

'Oh Grace, I'm sorry.' He sat up, held her face in his hands and kissed her gently, shifting to touch his lips to her eyelids one by one.

Declan's expression froze and he turned and faced the cat. 'It said I was a nice, gentle tom.'

Grace gaped at him. 'She did?'

Declan let Grace go. She went to the window and stroked Fel as she looked out into the yard. Grey wisps of mist were dissipating rapidly. Her gaze passed over Declan's bike, parked in the driveway. She remembered what he'd said. No gossip. Her eyes rolled. She had blabbed it all to her mother and Elena, but hey, he didn't own her and he'd never tried not telling Elvira anything, so bad luck.

'Um…I think if you wanted to keep this secret

you might have blown it. I mean, we might have blown it.'

Declan laid back on the bed, his head resting on his folded arms. 'Yeah. Who can keep sex with you secret? I'm sure they heard you in Marrickville on the other side of Sydney Harbor.'

'Hey, you made a bit of a commotion yourself.'

'I did at that.'

'So, are you up for breakfast? Mother has already sent her request in. Pancakes on the menu.'

'You got bacon?'

'We sure do.'

He rolled off the bed and started searching the floor for his clothes.

'Are you sure you're up to this? After all, it's my mother.'

'Sure, I can cope with Elvira. Elena and I are buddies from way back. So no problem there.'

'Fine. I'm going to clean up and start breakfast. You can make the coffee. Elena takes tea in the morning. And if you change your mind and feel like slinking away, I'll leave the window open.'

She ambled to the door, a smile plastered on her face. Declan for breakfast was a nice thought.

'Grace?' He swiveled his head from her to the window. 'I'm not a coward.'

She laughed at his wounded expression. 'We are talking about meeting my mother over the breakfast table, after you climbed in through my window and banged me senseless throughout the wee, small hours of the morning—noisily. If you think she'd let that go by without a comment or two, you're out of your senses. I'm just letting you know if you need an out, there is one and I'll forgive you.'

He weighed that up, stroking his chin as he stared at the window. 'Thanks, I think.'

'She is going to be impressed with those leathers.'
'Really?'
'I was.'
He picked up a pillow and tossed it.
Grace quickly shut the door, and giggled while she rested against it. With a sigh, she headed to the bathroom. There was a spring in her step and she did her best to keep her excitement down. There was no commitment. He enjoyed her as much as she did him, but he was determined not to settle down. All she could do was enjoy it while it lasted and try not to think about future heartbreak.

Her mother was bleary-eyed when she fronted at the table. Declan was making the coffee and her mother had not acknowledged him yet. *Bad sign*, Grace thought. Declan thumped over in his big bikie boots and placed a cup before her. 'Good morning, Elvira. I understand you like milk and two sugars in your coffee.'

Her mother lifted her gaze and looked him up and down. 'My, my, Declan Mallory. You have grown into a big lad.' She winked at him and then picked up her cup.

Grace nearly dropped the frying pan she was holding as she was transferring crispy bacon to a plate. Her mother had meant that double entendre. Damn her. She would spill the beans that she knew about their encounter in the Blue Mountains. As Grace scraped the bacon onto the platter, she knew that it was silly. Both her mother and Elena would have heard everything, so they didn't even have to use their imaginations.

Elena came out of her room, draped in a Japanese

blue and white *yukata* and yawned loudly. 'Morning. Hi Declan.' She yawned again. 'I'm glad you two had a good time.'

Grace blushed. 'I'm sorry if I woke you.'

Elvira put her cup down, leaned back in her chair and barked out a laugh. 'Woke me? Damnation, girl. How could anyone sleep through that? It wasn't just the noise—the emotions, the emanations coming from that room probably alerted every member of the folk in a five-mile radius.'

Declan's face paled. 'I didn't realize.'

'I'm sure you didn't. If you wanted to keep your little affair secret, then you've failed. Every tongue from here to Newcastle will be talking of it. It's not often you get fireworks like that with a joining, but it was a marvelous thing to behold.'

'Joining?' Declan sank into a seat. 'We weren't joining.'

Elvira spiked some bacon and slid it onto her plate. 'If you say so, Declan.'

'I do say so. Grace understands.'

'Does she? Excellent then. But convincing your parents that there's nothing "special" between you will take some doing, believe me.' Her mother looked up and eyed both of their shocked faces. 'Okay. So I'm exaggerating. I'm a little grumpy from having my sleep disturbed.'

Grace sat down at the table, blowing hair out of her mouth and sending her fringe fluttering. That was a relief. She surveyed the table before her. With all that activity, she was very hungry and breakfast conversation, while not quite as she'd planned and rather embarrassing, was stimulating her appetite. If her mother had more to dish out, she'd rather take it on a full stomach.

'Pass the syrup, would you, Elena?'

Elena was pouring maple syrup over her pancake stack. 'Here you go. Did you do any caramelized bananas?'

'No, we're out. I made raspberry coulis.' She passed it over.

'Okay then.' Elena cut into her stack and closed her eyes in delight.

Grace rapidly dissected her food, shoveling it in without bothering to talk much. Her hunger was a beast that needed feeding urgently. Declan took a while to relax after the first bit of conversation with her mother, but then after sipping his coffee, his plate began to fill. He stuck in. 'This is good,' he said around a mouthful of bacon.

'Thanks.'

Grace speared another pancake. She was almost full. Her mother got up for more coffee, so Grace handed up her cup. She needed extra fortification. Elena engaged Declan in conversation. She asked about his teaching and the adult classes he had planned. 'I wish I had talent enough to train. It sounds like fun.'

'Don't let that stop you, Ellie. Training of any kind is good.'

'Maybe, but I'm doing some craft classes at the local technical college. I have finally decided what I want to do with my life.'

Elvira's eyebrows rose as she sat down. 'That's good, dear. What is that exactly?'

'I like making things with my hands so I'm going to improve my skills and then set up a stall to sell things.'

Elvira was nodding. 'You could use your talent, too. Imbue them with health and happiness charms. I'm sure you'll be able to get permission to sell them to humans.'

Elena beamed. 'Then you approve?' She clapped her hands. 'That's wonderful, thank you. I thought you might be disappointed in me.'

Elvira waved her hand. 'Don't be ridiculous. I want you to be happy and fulfilled. If I've commented on your life, it was for that reason.'

Elena beamed at Grace and Declan. Grace could sense her happiness from where she sat. They had always been attuned.

The conversation lulled. Grace had to ask the question because she had a feeling that Declan would not bring it up himself. It was her family business. 'Mother, can you tell me about Uncle Elroy?'

Elena's head shot up. 'We have an Uncle Elroy?'

Elvira's gaze slid to Declan, instinctively knowing where Grace had heard the story. Elvira fiddled with her cutlery, not meeting Grace and Elena's gazes. She coughed once, then again, as if clearing her throat.

'It was a long time ago. I thought he would be forgotten by most.' She flicked her gaze at Declan. 'But I suppose never by some families.'

Grace's food was heavy in her gut. Declan reached over and covered her fist in his hand. She hadn't realized that she had been tense. It was bad, though. Her mother's vibrations were very low. This was going to be hard for her.

'He was younger than me, a half-brother, actually. And he was strange since birth. No one really understood why. Gifted and warped, he was.' Her gaze passed over Grace and centered on Declan.

'He liked to take life. Any life. It started with animals at first. Birds. Dogs. Cats. Then it was other children.'

Grace sucked in a breath. Her uncle had been a monster. 'Children?'

Elvira nodded. 'Yes. We didn't know about it at

first. The bodies turned up and we were stumped. Mace Denton, Mallory's cousin, was only young when he went missing. The whole coven went looking for him. Pris and I found them under the Harbor Bridge, late at night. We didn't like going there. All that iron and concrete interfered with the natural rhythms of the goddess. But that's where Mace's cries had drawn us. Elroy had tortured him, like he had the pets and the wildlife that were unfortunate enough to come into his path. He stood there in the shadows, just waiting, as if nothing terrible had happened.

'We called the coven. Elroy didn't even blink, didn't raise an eyebrow. It was as if the taking of life meant nothing to him. He was ten years old.'

'What happened to him, Aunt?' Elena asked in a hushed voice, tears glistening in her eyes.

'They sentenced him to death. It was unanimous.'

'But he was only a child himself,' Declan said.

Elvira squared up to him, shifting in her chair. 'You think that, do you? There was a lot of debate before and after. Was he an old, evil soul inhabiting a child's body? Was he just a warped soul never to be shaped into a useful member of the coven? We'll never know.'

'He's dead, then?' Grace asked. Her gut churned. It was all too much to process. Declan had known and hadn't said. His parents had known and had told him. His own uncle had been murdered as a child by her blood kin. How shocking.

'Yes, he's dead. But not executed. He killed himself.' Elvira closed her eyes. 'We were gathered in the great hall in Parramatta for the formal judgement. Elroy came along as if it were any other outing. He was called forth to receive judgement. When he took his place, he ripped his own…oh goddess…I can't.'

Elena got up and rubbed Elvira's shoulder. 'You don't have to if it distresses you.'

Elvira patted her hand and straightened her shoulders. 'I have to tell it now. Once a tale begins it must unravel to the end.' She cradled her head in her hand and took a deep, calming breath. Then she took a sip of coffee before lifting her head to continue the story. 'He used magic like a blade, split himself from nose to navel. There was so much blood. I vomited. So did many others. They performed the rituals to punish him in death as in life and then burned the remains. There, it is done. It is said. The monster killed himself.'

Grace sobbed into napkin. 'That's so horrible.'

'My mother said her brother was also killed.'

Elvira nodded. 'Yes, Saul. A lovely boy, so bright. Your mother never recovered from the shock. She found him, but there was nothing she could do. He died in her arms.'

Elvira's eyes clouded over with memories. None appeared to be good. How could Grace not have known this? They must have hidden it from her on purpose.

Grace trembled. Her mind spun down dark paths. It was as if her life was crumbling around her. Her uncle had killed two of Declan's family. How could he even sit in this room? It made so much sense now, why his parents had always been distant, that distance turning into hatred after she'd resurrected Fel. They feared the monster.

That monster was she. If Declan's parents thought that, then he must also think she was a monster. The recollection of his face when she'd raised Fel loomed large in her mind. The fear; the horror. Now that he knew what her uncle had done he'd be like them, hating her, thinking her a monster. Already he probably did.

Declan drew her head down to his shoulder, offering comfort. Grace couldn't rest there. She pulled back. Panic seized her. Her heart raced, her mind span. 'You knew about this?' Her voice was an accusatory hiss. 'You came here and slept with me, knowing this?' How could he? There must have been a good reason. He needed to get laid, wanted comfort and didn't want details getting in the way of that. How could he have done that, been intimate with her, then to tell her about her monstrous uncle?

'Now, Grace, wait a minute. Not the whole story. Just the part my parents told me. Their version.'

Grace sneered, her fists balled up hard. 'In what context?' Her voice was ranging high, but she was too angry and hurt to care. 'Don't worry, I can guess. They want to you to stay away from the taint, the dark magic-wielding evil witch.'

'Come on, Grace. Don't be like that.'

'You knew Elroy murdered children, didn't you? Before you raised the subject?'

Declan lowered his gaze to the table-top. The fat from his uneaten bacon congealing.

'Tell the truth. You knew he was a monster?'

He nodded, his Adam's apple bobbing as he swallowed. 'Perhaps I shouldn't have said anything.' He sought support from Elena and Elvira.

'So you were discussing me with your family. I'm a monster to them, too, aren't I?

His face paled and he kept his face neutral, but that expression spoke loudly. 'Grace—'

'It's true!' Hysteria had possession of her. How could he have mentioned it to her after their magical love-making? Couldn't he have waited for another time? What kind of jerk did that? He'd meant to hurt her.

Her gaze shifted to her mother. 'It's true, isn't it?' Her voice sliced into her mother. 'The coven think I'm another monster, don't they? When I raised Fel, it sent up warning flags. Beware, the Denholm clan has produced another monster. Beware.' Grace waggled her fingers.

Her mother kept her features very calm. Grace took that for a yes. 'Goddess, why didn't you tell me? All this time I thought I was atoning for my own misdeeds. Now, I find that there is a whole raft of other deeds, other evil deeds that I have to atone for. That I didn't even know about.'

'Grace, stop that. Stop that right now.' Her mother stood up, thumping the table.

'No, I won't stop. You should have told me.'

Elvira's gazed flicked to Declan. 'Don't do this now, Grace.'

Elena started crying, holding her hand over her mouth, her eyes wide with fright.

'You should have warned me.' Grace's voice now was a low hiss. 'How could I prepare? Battle something I didn't know existed?'

Grace was on her feet, her tears streaming down her face. Declan got out of her mother's way as she came around the table to Grace. The slap sent Grace's head to one side. 'Control yourself,' her mother said in a steady voice. 'You are not a monster. But you are being ridiculous.'

Grace ground her teeth and glared at her mother. 'How can you say that?'

'I know you, Grace.'

Her eyes passed over Declan's concerned face. It was so unfair.

'They think I'm a monster.' She threw her hand out, gesturing in the direction of Balmain.

'You have no control over other people's opinions. Elroy's legacy affects us all. There are so few warlocks now. Don't you understand?'

'No, I don't. How can I understand when I'm ignorant of the facts, facts other people know? Declan knows.' She caught a sob in her hand, shaking her head.

Declan put his hand on her back, stroked her. She shook him off. 'Don't touch me. Aren't you worried that you'll be tainted by a monster?'

Declan was quick to respond in anger. 'That's not fair. I only just heard about it last night. Don't judge me for what other people think. I'm not like that.'

She faced him, looked him up and down. 'You're just like them.' Anger she'd never experienced before overwhelmed her. It frightened her. She was a monster. The story of Elroy had let it out, had torn off the bandages holding the bad Grace in. 'Get out. Just get out and leave me alone.'

Her jaw clenched, and she fisted both hands by her side.

Declan paled and fell back a step. 'You don't mean that.' His gaze travelled all over her face. 'Don't do this. Please.'

'I do mean it. Just go. I never want to see you again. Take your superior battle mage demeanor and your upright family heritage and get out.' She spoke imperiously to Elvira. 'Mother, make him go.'

Elvira straightened her shoulders and looked down her nose, putting on her most displeased expression. Grace usually feared it but she was beyond that now. 'I'll do no such thing. You're being ridiculous.'

'Am I?' She glared at them all. 'Am I?'

Turning on her heel, she shoved a kitchen chair out of her way and then ran down the hall to her room.

Heavy footsteps followed her.

'Wait, Declan,' Elvira said. 'You best give her time to work it out. It's been a shock. Don't take what she said to heart. I've never seen her so upset.'

'I will wait,' came Declan's reply, his deep voice cutting through Grace's rage.

'It may take a while.' There was movement. 'There, there, Elena. It will be all right. Don't you worry. She'll be fine tomorrow.' Elena's weeping tormented Grace. She needed to shut them out.

Declan still hovered there. She could feel his presence. She was afraid he would try to talk to her, so she put up wards so he couldn't come in. Then she threw up additional ones so that she couldn't hear them any longer. She didn't want to hear them pity her or make excuses for her behavior. The wards would keep them out too, and would keep them from mentally communicating with her.

As she put the final touches on her wards, she locked the window and tugged the curtains so that there was no light. She stood in the darkness, misery enveloping her. Why had Declan told her about Elroy? Or why hadn't he explained it was that bad, given her some inkling? She'd had no comeback, no time to prepare. She blamed her mother, too, for not saying anything. She blamed Declan's parents. They'd done it to hurt her, to crush Declan's feelings for her.

Facing the door, she let the thoughts flow. It had been such a perfect morning. Now it was all over. Her life was over. Declan was over. No one in their right mind wanted to be with tainted goods. When she thought about it, Declan would give up on her. How could he not? He never had a commitment anyway. She was just for a good time. His parents had a valid reason for despising her. Given time, Declan would get over his rebellion against them; he'd give in to their wishes and settle down with some nice witch and have a family.

Grace was crazy to think she would get a life like that. She was from bad blood. Mating with her would just risk bringing more evil into the world. Then, giving over to her feelings, she sank to the floor and wept.

After an hour or so she lay on her back and stared at the ceiling. She needed more fuel, so she flicked on her music and filled the room with lyrics full of heartbreak, betrayal and mental anguish. There she screamed, letting her rage out. It was so unfair. Never had she voiced that thought before. She thought her punishment was deserved. Now she didn't agree. It was Elroy they were punishing. But she wasn't Elroy. They hadn't even lived in the same time period. Declan had hinted that there was something more. Grace furrowed her brow. What other ramifications were there?

Then it hit her. Her mother had said it, plain as day. There are so few warlocks because of Elroy. It was deliberate. The coven had been afraid that another Elroy would be born. They would have exiled his soul as a matter of course. But still the fear lived on. Wiping her nose with a towel she found on the floor, she remembered how frightened the coven had been when she'd brought back Fel, so casually, with so little effort.

She cried some more. Her tears would never end. Sometime later she woke to the sound of someone pounding on her door. She ignored them and crawled into bed. She'd set wards but they didn't prevent someone outside her room knocking. By then she was too exhausted to care and she didn't even re-member hearing the knocking stop.

❧

Declan's anger filled him up. How dare that stuck-up Elvira blast him for mentioning Elroy to Grace? Her words were still ringing in his ears. 'How could you do that to her? She loves you, always has.'

'I never asked her to love me and I certainly didn't promise her anything.'

Elvira had thrown up her hands. 'I don't think she knows she loves you, but you've hurt her bad, Declan Mallory. You and your family have a lot to answer for.'

'What do you mean? Seems to me that they're the victims.'

Elvira had scoffed. 'Victims. Always first to cast the first stone, and you're just like them. Your mother always did have a slim grip on reality. She—'

'Don't bring my mother into this. What has she ever done to you?'

Elvira had thrown up her hands. 'No family is perfect. Show me the perfect family. We all have de-fects and skeletons in the closet. Why don't you ex-plore yours before you come over here and destroy the happiness of such a beautiful person like Grace? Knowing her, knowing her spirit, how could you crush her so?'

'Me? I didn't. I have no idea what you're talking about. I just asked a question.'

'If you don't see it then just get out. You are too stupid even to talk to.'

Fist balled, Declan had spun on the spot. 'I will.'

He'd ground his teeth and clenched his jaw against the words he'd wanted to yell at that old witch.

How dare she heap all the blame on him? He had only wanted to unwind with Grace, enjoy her body, and enjoy her smile and her wit. He hadn't asked for all this drama to be dumped on him.

Declan had stormed out the front door. He'd tried contacting Grace as he left, but her wards kept him out. He shook his head. The whole family were nutters, except maybe Elena, who had sat there crying and gaping at them all.

Declan had jogged to his bike, revved it up and sped off. He drove for hours and hours, only turning back when he hit Newcastle. Now, many hours later he stood outside his front door. With his hands in his pockets, he kicked at a stone on the path, not quite ready to face his parents. His stomach rumbled. He hadn't eaten since breakfast. No point in stalling any longer. He could smell roast meat.

His parents looked up from the kitchen table as he walked in. 'Hello, son. Glad you're home.'

'You've seen her again, haven't you?' his mother said, screwing up the tea towel she held in her hands. 'I can smell her on you.'

'Del.' His father's warning was soft, gentle.

Her head jerked in his direction. 'I can taste her taint from here. Go wash her off. You won't be eating at my table until you do.'

'Mum. Don't. It's been a bad day.'

'What happened?' his father asked.

'I asked about Elroy Denholm. Let's just say I'm not welcome there anymore.'

'You see? He was there. He went to her.'

His father stood and went to cuddle his mother. 'Let it go now. He's back. It's over. She won't get him. It's ended,' he cooed to Declan's mother. Declan's stomach roiled and he slammed the door as he left the room. He needed to shower and he needed time alone. Elvira's words were still in his ears. He didn't like looking at his mother and seeing what was obvious. He'd ignored the signs his whole life. He'd been brought up not to upset her. To bring his troubles to his father and not bother his mother.

Damn Elvira Denholm. Damn her for being right. His bloodline wasn't perfect either.

❀

Grace awoke before dawn, her mouth dry, and she was busting to pee. Was the coast clear? Could she get to the bathroom before she was intercepted?

Lowering her wards, she hesitated, waiting for a shrill mind scream from her mother, but there was nothing. As she opened the door a crack she saw no one in the hallway and darted out, tripping over Elena who was asleep on the floor.

'Grace,' she said in hushed tones. 'Please talk to me.'

Grace disentangled herself from Elena's long legs, shaking her head. She turned and scrambled into the bathroom, groaning with relief when she made it inside. After relieving herself, she stared at her reflection in the mirror. Her hair was a scramble and her eyes so puffy she looked as if she'd been punched. Leaning over the sink, she splashed her face and then drank deeply, direct from the tap. Her gaze shot to the window. Should she climb out so she didn't have to face Elena or her mother? That was a bit of overkill as she'd have to climb back inside, and as she had lowered her wards, they could very well be sitting on her bed waiting for her.

Closing her eyes, she sighed and then hiccuped. Elena had been quiet; maybe she would be again. Using a hand towel, she scrubbed her face dry. It was time she faced what her family were going to throw at her.

Elena haunted the hallway but backed away from Grace's determined step.

'Please, talk to me,' she whispered.

Grace kept walking, shut the door in Elena's face and locked it. The sound of her cousin putting her head against the door brought on another fit of weeping. Grace lay on the bed, three pillows over her head to muffle the sound. She hurt so much; it was as if her life were aching. It was as if all the wrongs that had been done to her were experienced again and mourned over.

The day came and went. Grace stared at the ceiling. Although she hadn't eaten, she wasn't hungry. Someone suddenly pounded on the door. 'Grace Riordon, you open this door and drop your wards right now.' It was her mother and she wasn't pleased. Her mother was a powerful witch, but Grace wasn't that bad either. She was pretty certain her ward would withstand an assault. 'Grace, I'm warning you. Do not put your health at risk. You have to come out and eat something.'

Grace continued to stare at the ceiling. A thrust of magic against her ward had her gasping for breath. Her ward held but she could tell her mother was very upset. On one level Grace was sorry to cause her so much worry, but she was hurting so bad she couldn't acknowledge it.

She drifted off to sleep as night fell. Around midnight there was an urgent knocking on the door. 'Please, Grace. Don't do this to me.' It was Elena, her voice clogged with tears. 'I need you like I need light.'

Her nails clawed the door. 'You are my light. Your suffering makes us all suffer. Don't shut me out. Please, Grace, don't shut me out. You're everything to me. We are sisters of the soul.'

Tears leaked out of Grace's eyes and she nodded silently, biting on her bottom lip. With the back of her hand, she wiped her eyes. It was true she and Elena had a special bond. Elena's words cut through the self-loathing and self-pity she was wallowing in. Dropping her ward, she reached out and knew that Elena was suffering as much as she was.

She rolled off the bed and stared at the door, hesitating before confronting her cousin. It was a moment of no return. Before she could move, Elena flung open the door and stood on the threshold, her face stained with tears and her hair unbrushed. Her green irises were very bright, given the redness of her eyes.

Grace held out her arms and Elena raced forward. With a flick of magic, she shut the door tight. It wasn't that she was punishing her mother; she was just punishing her mother.

Elena clung to her and wept. Grace stroked her hair and rocked her back and forward. After a few minutes, Elena calmed down. 'I'm sorry. I should be comforting you. Everything was going so well and then that bombshell hit.'

'Tell me about it.'

'Your mother is very distressed. Her and Declan had a big fight and he stormed off, saying he'd never come back again. Elvira was very down on his mother, hinting that she was loopy. After Declan left, she told me Delores had never been the same after the murder. She never got over her grief. None really understood the why of it.

'I'm afraid Declan didn't take it too well—the implication that his mother wasn't quite right in the head.'

Grace sighed, heavy with grief. She wanted it all to go away.

'You know the reason we have so few warlocks is due to Elroy too.'

Elena nodded. 'I feel so sorry for you all though,' Elena said, with a sniff. 'Such a tragic business.'

Grace lay down on the bed. 'What makes me angry is that they've not forgotten any of it, but didn't tell us, the younger generation, you know? They're putting pressure on us to reproduce, to swell the coven's ranks when it was their own behavior that caused the gender imbalance. There must be two witches for every warlock.'

Elena put her head down on the pillow and sniffed loudly. 'Not quite two. But a nice warlock, who is okay-looking and not an ass, is virtually impossible to find. You mother said it wasn't only the Elroy incident that affected the birth-rate. Some members of the coven have drifted away to mingle with humans. Like my mother, I suppose. It's only luck Elivra found me.'

'Not luck. She looked for you. Sniffed you out with her witch sense. Oh, Elena. I can't face it. I really can't. How can I go out there knowing everyone is waiting for me to turn into a monster?'

Elena grinned. 'A monster? Is that what you think?'

'Well, yes.'

Elena rolled over and played with Grace's hair. 'The Mallorys have always been strange—the parents, I mean, not Declan. Some of the other old sticks are a bit odd, and maybe they are a bit wary. But the rest of us, you know the people our age don't know about this Elroy and wouldn't care. The reason you get flack from other young witches is because you're competition.'

'Competition?'

'Yes, exactly. I get a little bit of snub from them now and again, but I'm a half-witch so I'm not a threat.' She poked Grace on the sternum. 'You, though, are beautiful, have an amazing spirit full of joy and love, which you can't repress, and you're a powerful witch as well. In other words, hot property. They can't compete.'

Grace lay back and closed her eyes, letting her breath out slowly. She was numb on the inside. She wasn't about to argue with Elena. 'Thank you for the kind words.'

'Grace, stop that. They aren't "kind" words. Sense me, please. Know what I feel about you.'

Grace shook her head. 'I don't want to.'

Elena grabbed her hand. 'I never took you for a coward. I'm offering to share my heart with you; don't push me away. I couldn't bear it. You've been my light, my beacon. You accepted me when I came here. For the first time in my life I truly belonged—you gave me that.'

'I'm in a dark place…I can't get out.'

'Nonsense. You refuse to even try.'

Grace rolled onto her side, turning her back on Elena, who laid there, breathing and saying nothing.

A light touch caressed her mind. Grace blinked. That wasn't Elena reaching out to her? Not possible. She flipped over. Elena sat very still, eyes closed, breathing regulated. The feather touch reached out again, stronger. Grace couldn't stop herself from reciprocating. Then next second she was inside Elena, surrounded by her love, her images of Grace from when they were teenagers, the special moments Elena had cherished and stored away.

Silent tears dampened Grace's cheeks. Closing her own eyes, Elena's presence filled her up, cocooned her in joy. Those dark tendrils of shame and anger dropped away and Grace could once again touch hope and love.

Another set of arms embraced them. Elvira. Her mother sobbed as she caressed their heads, soothed their unruly hair.

'My girls. Oh, my girls. Thank the goddess.'

An hour or so later they let each other go. Elvira held out her arms. 'Forgive me.'

Grace's smile teased her face. 'Mother, there's nothing to forgive. You didn't know Declan's mother would bring it up.'

'I should've predicted it. What kind of witch am I?'

Grace shook her head. 'Out of practice with that lot. They have been in the UK for a long time.'

Elvira looked up, her eyes widening slightly. 'You're right. I am out of practice.' She looked her up and down. 'I think a shower for you and then a hot meal.'

Grace nodded. 'Okay, but—'

'You don't want to go out.' She nodded. 'Take your time. I'll go and cook something. Stroganoff maybe, although I can't make it as well as you.' She lifted herself off the bed and headed for the door.

'About Declan.'

Elvira paused and looked back over her shoulder. 'Yes.'

'It was never a joining, Mother. He won't come back. Not after what happened.'

'I have a confession to make. I banned him from the house.'

Grace jolted her head back. 'Including in the house wards?' Being one of the folk, he could come to their house without permission as Elvira was on the council.

Elvira tilted her head to the side and grinned. 'Not quite made it to the wards yet.'

Grace was certain Declan would never come back, not in the same way. But maybe in a month or two when she got over their break-up, she'd be able to meet him as an acquaintance.

'Don't bother going to any trouble on my account. He won't be back. Not after that hysterical display.'

Her mother winked. 'If you say so, dear. You were rather impressive.'

CHAPTER FIVE

About a month after the dramatic altercation with Grace, Declan arrived home later than expected. He'd been training the adult folk for a month now. Word had it that Grace Riordon hadn't left her house in all that time. Couldn't leave her house due to some illness. When he'd run into Elena, he'd been assured that everything was okay and that it was nothing serious. Grace needed time; that was all.

Elena had accepted an invitation to have coffee with him. It didn't escape Declan's notice that there were three witches who took seats in the café after they sat down. He was still hot property apparently. *Still being stalked.*

'You should join my course. It will be good for you.'

'Yes, I know I should, but I'm really enjoying these craft lessons I'm doing. I feel my goal to look after myself, financially and otherwise, is getting closer. The time conflicts.'

'Look, okay. How about I give you one-on-one tuition?'

Elena shrugged. 'That's a great idea, but where? Home isn't really appropriate right now.'

Declan thought about his place and considered it wasn't worth the hassle with his parents. 'Leave it with me and I'll get back to you.'

'Thank you.'

They sat in companionable silence, sipping coffee, each thoughtful.

Suddenly, Elena squeezed his hand. He started as he'd been distracted for some minutes. Elena's coffee cup was empty. 'I've got to head off now. Take care.' Her gaze traveled around the café, noting the other witches. She turned and smirked at him.

'They are persistent.'

He nodded. 'Catch you later. I'll let you know about those lessons.'

After, Declan ordered more coffee and ignored his fan club. It was past seven before he received an urgent hail from his father. *Where are you? We had a dinner tonight. Special, you know. Your mother went to a lot of trouble.*

Sorry, I'll be there shortly, Declan sent back.

Declan rolled his eyes. That's right, his parents had invited Danila over for a family meal. He was being offered up on a plate to the witch they most admired. Pity Danila was a shallow creature with a nasty streak. He hadn't forgotten how she'd tried to get Grace into trouble by sneaking that ugly blouse into her bag.

The food had been laid out by the time he'd arrived home and washed up. 'Sorry for being late.' Danila simpered at him as he took his seat. 'You look stunning, tonight, Danila.'

He had to admit she had gone to a lot of trouble. She was tastefully made up, her hair curled so it fell invitingly around her shoulders and down her back.

Her halter dress appeared to be staying on with a bow. It was a floral dress in blues and greens, and did nothing to enhance her slight figure.

'Good to see you again. You are so hard to find.' She leaned down, giving him a healthy view of her breasts through the gap in the top of her dress. Deliberate, he thought.

'I'm not hard to find. You saw me at battle class tonight.'

'That's not what I meant. You're not easy to get alone.'

Declan lifted a mocking eyebrow. 'I'm not a battle mage for nothing. Excuse me.' He leaned over and skewered some meat.

Danila faced him a little longer and then leaned back to start her own meal. 'Just vegetables for me, if you don't mind, Dee.'

Declan paused and without lifting his head caught his father's eye. *Dee?* He sent a quick message.

Yes, they got cosy earlier, was his father's response.

Declan didn't miss the way his father's cheeks reddened. *So he damn well should be embarrassed, trying to match-make.* He'd explained his position to his father. He'd thought it was agreed upon. How many ways could you say 'no matchmaking'?

With a grunt, Declan kept on filling his plate. Danila was making a fuss and providing herself with a small serving. He rolled his eyes. He preferred women with appetites and with figures that could cope with some rough handling. Danila had arms like sticks.

The food was good and once his hunger was assuaged, his mood mellowed a bit. His mother kept up a running dialogue with Danila, offering to show her pictures of him when he was young. Declan didn't bite when Danila said she was dying to see them.

After dessert, they went into the lounge room. The conversation sagged. Declan wasn't interested and the sound of his mother raving about him, his looks and his accomplishments, made him grit his teeth. What was she doing? Trying to sell him off to the highest bidder? He was perfectly capable of finding his own woman if he wanted one.

Eventually, he cracked under pressure. 'Mum. Mum! Can you stop? I'm sure Danila has heard enough about me. Why don't we talk about her?'

His mother stiffened. 'I'm only trying to help.'

'I don't need help. Neither does Danila.'

'I don't mind the help, Dee.' But she giggled and that did the trick.

'Stop calling her that,' Declan snapped.

His mother sucked in a breath. 'Oh my dear. I feel faint. Please help me.' His mother began a slow glide to the floor. His father caught her, soothed her as she moaned loudly.

'Come on, dear. You need to lie down. You've been slaving in the house all day. No, no, don't mind him. He's moody. He'll apologize later, you'll see.'

Declan resisted muttering under his breath. Despite losing his patience, she was his mother and he loved her and tolerated her foibles to a high degree. He was reluctant to acknowledge some deeper issue, as Elvira had suggested.

His father led his mother to their room, which left Declan sitting alone with Danila.

He shrugged, avoiding meeting her eyes. 'Well, I'm sorry about that. I put a bit of a damper on the evening. Should I show you out?'

Danila coughed and he looked at her. She smiled and sat back on the easy chair she was sitting in. 'I wasn't thinking of leaving just yet. But it's a lovely night. Perhaps a stroll in the backyard would be nice.

I believe the jasmine is in blossom. I was out there earlier for the tour.'

Declan chewed the inside of his cheek. They had a very small suburban garden. His parents were not into it at all. Their dream garden was the one they'd focus on when they retired. But he'd already upset one woman that evening so he bowed her ahead of him and followed her outside.

It was a three-quarter moon and despite Sydney's pollution, it provided sufficient light to see Danila. 'Not much out here to see,' he said, casting his gaze around the yard. A few shadowy lumps of bushes were all that could be seen.

'What about this?'

He turned back. In the glow of the backlight, Danila stood with her dress undone and pooled around her feet. She wore no underwear. 'Danila...'

She stepped in close, picked up his right hand and placed it on her breast. She groaned with feigned pleasure. Surely, she knew he could tell she was faking it.

'Oh Declan.' She threw her head back, eyes closed. 'Just the feel of you touching me is turning me on.' Her voice was low and husky. 'Take me now. Be my first love.'

Declan rolled his eyes and pinched her nipple.

'Ow.' She opened her eyes and glared at him.

'You know I'm not interested in being your first love, which is an out-and-out lie. I can smell the human you were screwing before you got here. Put your dress on. You're wasting time with me.'

'I haven't been with a human.'

'Really? Then who were you screwing in the bushes before battle class this evening? I get there an hour beforehand to meditate and practice. However,

I had trouble concentrating because of your chosen root's mating noises.'

She crouched to bring up her dress. 'You're a real jerk, Declan Mallory,' she said with feeling as she fumbled with the ties of her dress.

'Yes, I really am.'

'We could have been great.' She tried to do up her dress but the halter dropped, exposing her breasts. 'You could have enjoyed these.'

He was feeling pretty nasty at that moment, really wanting to be left alone. 'I've had better.'

With a cry, she turned and ran into the house, yelling up a storm. He heard his father's deeper tones, concern evident in his voice. He wouldn't be surprised if Danila accused him of rape.

Declan lowered himself onto the back step, letting the cool fingers of the night air calm his hot temper. He'd had better than Danila. He'd had better than all the others who kept flinging themselves at him. He'd had Grace.

'You look lovely, Grace,' her mother said when she appeared in the lounge room, dressed formally for the joining feast. Fern Primscomb had snared Ambrose Fullworth, and that was cause for celebration.

Actually, it was an excuse to get her out of the house and after six weeks or so of moping, Grace needed air. She was sufficiently restored to meet Declan Mallory again, with more indifference than previously.

No gossip had reached her. Both Elvira and Elena had not bothered even to mention his name, let alone who he might be dating or joining with. There were plenty of candidates. She had to move beyond that.

'Wow, that looks fab!' Elena said as she came in. 'Cream does suit your complexion, and those pleats make you look like a depiction of the goddess.'

Grace twirled, liking how the skirt flared out. The gold chain under the breast of the empire line did make her appear like something of the goddess. Her dark hair had been elaborately curled and threaded through with flowers and clipped up high, giving her neck a longer line. She looked ready to face the world, and more importantly, ready to face Declan and his family.

'Come along, girls. Time to make an entrance.' Elvira was full of energy and excitement. She always did get a buzz out of coven events. Grace and Elena, less so. Mostly because there wasn't much to look at in the warlock stakes, and if there was, there were too many other girls to compete with.

Elena had coupled with a few humans—young, lusty males who she sent packing after a short time. It didn't work out, having to hide half her life. With a wry smile, Grace understood that they both had issues with the opposite sex.

Both of them shared a sense of unworthiness, though coming from different sources. Then again, they both had the same relatives. In order not to upset herself, Grace changed the direction of her thoughts. There was no point in thinking about events she had no control over, no point regretting a past that was long gone.

Elvira drove them to the community hall where the joining feast was to be held. The ride was smooth in Elvira's new car, a sleek midnight-blue Commodore. There was a moment of apprehension when Grace heard the sounds of laughter coming from the hall as she opened the car door. She closed her eyes and mentally prepared herself to face people again.

Her mother expected more from Grace than cringing before her peers and embarrassing her in front of the coven, of which she'd worked hard to be one of the leaders. Grace tightened the laces on her emotions and climbed out of the car.

Once in the hall, the bubble and crash of noise and people was overwhelming at first. Grace tried not to appear chickenhearted, even though she kept behind her mother as she threaded her way through the crowd, searching for her cronies.

Elena slipped her arm through hers and led her off to a corner before Elvira had reached her goal—a group of coven council members. 'We don't want to get stuck with that lot. We'd never get away.'

With a laugh, Grace patted Elena's hand. 'You're right. I forgot about that technicality.' With Elena sheltering her from view, she stood in the corner, looking at the crowd but not actually seeing it. 'You think you can score me a drink?'

'Sure, I think sparkling wine tonight. I'm feeling bubbly and happy because well…just because.'

Grace grinned at her and waved her away. 'Hurry, I need that drink.' When Elena disappeared into the crowd, Grace composed herself, trying not to meet anybody's eye. She was here, but not socializing. Being there was enough effort for one evening.

A familiar voice reached her.

'Grace?' Declan walked up to her. 'You look amazing.'

Grace didn't want to look into his eyes so she kept her gaze lowered. 'Thank you.' She hoped he would go away, hoped Elena would come back quickly.

Declan didn't walk away as she'd expected he

would. She lifted her head and saw him studying her, a smile on his face, genuine interest in his gaze.

Music started up, the beautiful flowing notes of a flute, the rhythmic beat of a drum. A violin started, adding its clear notes to the melody.

Declan edged closer. 'Will you dance with me, Grace?'

She opened her mouth, but nothing came out. With a large smile, he encircled her with his arms and drew her into the dance. Their movements were slow and sensual. He held her lower back so that she pressed against him, whether she wanted to or not. She could scarcely pull her wits together. Being this close had her thoughts in broken bits. She couldn't assemble them.

She'd not expected him to want to speak to her, let alone dance with her in front of everyone. They danced in front of his parents. Grace looked away but not before she caught the look of hate on his mother's features. It really was too much.

They'd angled round the floor near to where she'd first been standing. 'Please can we stop now?'

Declan lifted his head and put distance between them. He studied her face. 'If you're sure.' He went to walk away and paused. Running his hand through his hair, he said, 'Look, Grace, I wanted to apologize for what happened, for my part in it.'

Grace couldn't look at him. Her heart was thumping loudly, her stomach coiled with tension. 'It's okay. You don't need to say anything.'

He leaned in close, kissing her on the ear lobe. 'I've missed you. It's so good to see you again.' Those dark eyes glinted as they studied her face.

There was a cough behind them and Declan swung round. 'Elena. You look fantastic. I love the whole peasant look.'

Elena laughed. She turned around, letting her peasant skirt flow out while keeping the contents of the two champagne glasses she held in place. 'I made it myself.'

Grace's jaw dropped. 'You did?' How had she missed that?

'Yes, I made it in my craft class. I've taken an option to learn how to sew and it's so much fun.' She passed over a glass of champagne.

Grace took the champagne gratefully and gulped down half of it. Her nerves were getting the better of her. They both kept their gazes on Declan and he shrugged. 'Best be going. I can see your mother heading this way.'

Declan disappeared into the crowd. Elena scanned the room, keeping a look out for him. After a few minutes, she observed, 'He wasn't going to get away that easy. Elvira has cornered him by the bar.' Elena clinked glasses with Grace and then laughed.

'What's so funny?'

'Life in general,' Elena replied.

Grace nodded, taking another sip of her wine. A few other acquaintances waved and headed in their direction. She couldn't deal right then. 'Can you excuse me for a minute, Elena?'

'Sure,' Elena said, lifting lifted her glass in a salute. 'I'll catch up with you later.'

Grace kept on the edge of the room, working her way around the crowd, only occasionally having to divert around a table full of witches and warlocks chatting away animatedly. She stopped by the bar to get a refill of her sparkling wine. It was there she felt a hard tap on the shoulder. 'Yes?' She turned around to be brought up short by Delores Mallory. Declan's mother grasped her elbow and dragged her to the back door. Grace clung to her glass, hoping not to lose all the contents.

Dumbfounded, Grace didn't have the wits to wrench her arm free. Delores let her go when they reached their destination, a quiet room. His mother leaned in close. 'Stay away from my son, you tainted cow.'

Putting distance between them, Grace took two mouthfuls of wine and placed the glass on a nearby table, readying her thoughts. 'I am staying away from your son.'

'It didn't look that way to me. Before you try for him again you should know he is with Danila now. They are going to join with each other. He had her naked on our back lawn just the other night.'

'How nice for you all. It's got nothing to do with me. I understood that Declan didn't want to settle down, but if he's changed his mind, I'm happy for you all. Now, if you've got nothing else to say, I would like to re-join my family.'

Grace turned away. 'You come from bad blood,' Delores shouted. 'You'll never be good enough for my son. You'll never be good enough for any warlock. I'm glad the line dies out with you.'

Shaken by the vitriol in her words, Grace ran out the back door instead of joining Elena. She had no time to find her mother and was too upset to hail her.

She ran down the long drive and smack into the back of Declan. He spun and caught her before she fell. 'Are you hurt?'

Grace had banged her nose. Drops of blood spanned the skirt of her dress. 'Don't touch me. I've had enough of you and your horrible family.' She burst into tears.

Declan had a hold of her and wouldn't let go.

'What are you saying? What's happened?' He glanced up the drive to the hall then back at her.

'Can't you leave me alone? She told me you're joining with Danila and I don't care. I don't care that you had her naked on the back lawn. I don't care how many of those bitch-witches you fornicate with, I just want to be left alone.'

She pushed out a surge of magic and he let go, leaving her to continue her flight down the driveway and out onto the road. Leaning over, she took deep breaths until she calmed enough to hail her mother. She wanted to be taken home.

By the time the car cruised down the driveway Grace was in control of herself, although she still wanted to leave. Elvira did a double-take when Grace slid into the front seat but said nothing. Elena was less restrained. 'What happened to you?'

They were wondering about the blood on her dress. 'It was just an accident. I couldn't stay in there with blood on my dress.'

'I guess not,' Elena commented from the back seat. Grace noted the look her mother shared with Elena. They both knew she could have spelled it off in a flash.

Grace was past caring what they thought. Rubbing at her upper arms, she stared out the window, trying not to think about what a bad idea it had been to come out. Part of her cherished that moment in Declan's arms, knowing that he had forgiven her in some small way. But his mother, she was beyond cruel. She wanted to hurt, and hurt Grace deep. That was repulsive to her on every level.

They remained in silence all the way home. Grace wanted to go straight to bed, but Elvira pressed her to drink a cup of hot chocolate. They were quiet, but she knew they would talk about her after she'd gone to sleep. Both of them had seen her dancing with Declan.

❀

Declan took long strides down the driveway, heading into the hall. He didn't know what had upset Grace but the change in her demeanor from when he'd danced with her until she'd bumped into him was so pronounced, he suspected that either Danila or his mother had said something to her. When he got to the door, his father was waiting. 'Do you mind driving us home? Your mother is not well.'

Declan chomped down on the angry retort he was about to let fly. 'Sure, I'll go get the car.'

When he pulled up, his father assisted his mother into the back seat and then slid in beside her. It must be bad, he thought. Although his father was very attentive when his mother had one of her spells, he usually let her sit in the back on her own.

Declan looked in the rear-vision mirror. 'Are you are right, Mother? I'll get you home soon.'

'Bad blood!' she hissed, then spat. Declan's eyes widened. 'She's a monster with bad blood. She even looks like him. Same eyes. Same skin.' His mother looked up, her face transformed by a twisted mouth and bulging eyes. Her voice rose in pitch. 'The same evil, ugly, dark hair.'

Fear trembled in Declan's gut. His turned his head towards his father, who was stroking his mother's head, whispering soothing words. 'Dad?'

His father shook his head. 'Don't listen to her, son.' Their gazes locked. 'Seeing the Riordon woman shocked her. Wasn't expecting to, I'm guessing.'

'Grace?'

'I told her,' she began to chant. 'She can't have

him, she can't. He had Danila on the lawn. I saw
them. I saw her naked. She can't have him. He's
joining with Danila.'

'Dad? What is going on?'

His father shook his head, his jaw slack with surprise. 'Er...I believe there must have been a con-
frontation.'

'You bet there was. I bumped into Grace. She
could barely speak she was so shaken.'

His mother continued to chant. None of it was
making any sense, but he guessed what had happened. His mother's wishes and dreams for him had
all twisted up with her hate. 'You need to get her seen
to, Dad. She is not well.'

'She is convinced that Danila is the one for you.
Can't you consider it, for her sake?'

Declan turned around and stared out the wind-
screen. The suggestion shocked him. Deep down he
knew he couldn't do it, no matter the loyalty and the
love he had for his family. He couldn't give up his future happiness like that.

He didn't want to settle down just yet and he really didn't like Danila. There was no connection, no
joy in being with her. She was like some sucking
vine, with the potential to drain the life and hope
from him. He shook his head. He wasn't normally
driven to such lengths, but he had a real aversion to
that woman. He sucked in a breath, deep into his
lungs. Danila had been unbearably cruel to Grace.
That was the first cut of dislike and it only got worse
at each encounter, until he had an open, festering
wound where that witch was concerned.

'I hate that witch with a vengeance. I'd rather be
celibate and live in a cave until my dying day than
join with her.'

His father spluttered. 'Steady on. What's got into you?'

Their eyes met through the rear-view mirror. 'Dad, I have no feeling for that stupid little witch that mother's taken a fancy to. She's shallow and nasty. More importantly, I will choose my own mate.' He gripped the steering wheel. 'I've told you both and I'm telling you again, I don't want to settle down yet. I have other plans. One day I'll have kids. But not now—not because you want me to. If I want to join with a woman, it will be because I want to, because I love her and want to be with her. Can't you understand that?'

His father coughed. Declan's eyes slid to his mother. She was out of it, eyes unfocused, mumbling away incoherently. 'Yes, son. I do understand.' He drew his wife to his shoulder and she relaxed, breathing deeply. Declan reached out with his senses and saw that his mother slept. His father spoke in hushed tones. 'I joined with your mother because it was how things were done in those days. Parents and the coven decided who would be together. I've stayed with her because she can't exist on her own. She needs me. She needs you.'

Declan threw his head back, hitting the headrest. 'Dad, you have to get some help for her. There's got to be something that can be done to help soothe her mind. I have to tell you now that I'm wise to the emotional blackmail. I've lived with it for years, but here and now I draw the line. You, both of you, stop meddling in my affairs and leave Grace Riordon alone.'

'You can't be serious. After all we've done for you.'

Declan let out a sigh. 'I'm perfectly serious. We're heading for a major breach here. If I walk away I won't come back. You get her seen to.

His father reached through from the back seat and clasped him on the shoulder. 'But I need your help. I can't do this on my own.'

Declan started the car and headed for home. He gripped the steering wheel so hard his wrists ached. It was as if he hadn't spoken. Was his father as far gone as his mother? The future looked bleak. His heart was heavy with guilt, love and duty.

By rights he should go to Grace and apologize for what his mother had said. He didn't want to give rise to expectations with her family. Elvira had warned him not to break her daughter's heart. If you're not serious, she'd said, stay away.

He cursed under his breath as he took the corner and then braked suddenly as a stray dog ran across the road. He cared for Grace, deeply. More deeply than he'd realized until he'd seen her so distressed. Yet he wasn't ready to commit.

CHAPTER SIX

Grace lay awake for most of the night. Every sound had her springing off the pillow and her gaze to the window. He wasn't coming. He wasn't coming to soothe her hurt or say sorry for his mother. He wasn't coming to tell her that the story about him and Danila was a lie. Scenes of him making love to Danila in the dark, under the moon, with the scent of grass in the air played out in her mind, Danila's long, blonde hair dancing against her back as he thrust into her.

'Stop that!' she grated against the pillow, her fists clenched tight. 'Stop tormenting yourself.'

As she fought her emotions, fought the disappointment, she knew it had to stop. No more angst, no more drama. She had to get back her equilibrium, restore order to her mind and stop upsetting those she loved. As the morning sun speared through the windows, Grace was sitting on the bed, ready to start the day.

With a look in her mirror, she saw that the slight bruising that had come out around her eyes was fading and the self-healing she'd administered had dispersed the pain. She ran a finger down her nose.

All good, as far as she could tell. No break. She checked the date. It was a teaching day. She sent off a hail to the head witch, letting her know that she was happy to take the class. The reply was rather tetchy. Grace giggled into her hand. It was 5.30 a.m. *Oops.*

After taking a shower, she sat at the kitchen table and had her lesson planned before her mother or Elena stumbled into the room. The aroma of coffee had lured them there.

'Grace?'

'Morning. I made an omelette. Coffee is ready. I'll be teaching this morning, so is there anything you want me to do on the way home?'

Elvira poured a cup of coffee, sugared it and then nursed it in her palm. 'It's way too early to be thinking.'

'Are you up to cooking for us tonight?' Elena asked.

Grace took a sip of her own coffee and then sighed with delight. 'I am. You want my special?'

Elena nodded. 'Sure do.'

'Mexican feast, sure thing. I'll pick up all the ingredients on the way home.'

Elena sat down next her. 'Great.' Then as Elvira headed to the bathroom, Elena leaned her head against Grace's. 'I'm so glad you are feeling better.'

'Me too.'

Her students were very cooperative that day. The smell of fresh-baked bread filled the classroom. They had made No Prove Bread and fresh butter. Not waiting for the bread to rise a second time meant they could complete the lesson during class. A bit of help from Grace in speeding things up also made sure the families got to taste the freshly prepared food. The butter had been churned with sour cream and joy; the bread kneaded with good health balm, enough to lift the eater's spirits. It was all gentle magic and fun for the class.

Although she wasn't looking forward to bumping into Declan, she was a bit surprised that he wasn't teaching the older children that day. As usual her pupils took all her attention, and she was quite surprised when the first parent came to collect their child. For the next twenty minutes she was saying goodbye, chatting to parents and tidying the room.

Pat Leahy, the head witch, came in before she left. 'It's good to have you back, Grace. The children missed you and your gentle magic.'

Grace looked up from groping in her cavernous handbag for her keys. 'It's good to be here. They were particularly well-behaved today.'

She picked up her handbag from the desk, the sack of leather that held a goodly portion of her possessions, and shook it, hoping to dislodge her car keys.

'Declan won't be around for a while.'

Grace stilled and lowered her handbag to the desk. 'Why? Has he given up teaching the children already?' She didn't mean for that to sound waspish. She chewed her lip and faced Pat.

The head witch shook her head. 'They've taken Delores to the Blue Mountains. There's a healer up there. Apparently, she had a bit of a meltdown at the joining celebrations the other night.'

With raised eyebrows, Grace nodded, trying not to let on that she was hurt or surprised by the news. 'I'm sorry to hear Declan's mother is not well. I hope things improve. The children liked his lessons.'

Grace turned back to her bag and used a little

spell. The keys leaped into her palm. Pat moved toward her, hand outstretched, pausing before actually touching her. 'Declan asked me to relay to you his regrets about anything his mother might have said to you. He asked me to assure you that she wasn't herself.'

Grace's eye widened. 'I…er…I'm not—'

The other witch smiled. 'I best let you go. Pierre will be here soon to run the adult class on medieval magical history.'

Grace cast a glance around the room and then said goodbye. By the time she reached her car, her knees were shaking. Hearing a message from Declan had disturbed her calm and she wasn't sure why. Did he know what his mother had said? Or was his mother really ill? The only way to find out was to ask her own mother, because as one of the council, she'd know an important detail like that.

Grace sat in the car, watching the leaves jostling in the wind. Patchy cloud blocked out the sun now and then. She hadn't put the key in the ignition. Declan's message had unsettled her and she didn't know how to react. She'd been so damn sure that it was over, that there was nothing and no point. Yet, his message blasted that surety as if he'd driven a pellet through a target. Did it mean that his mother was mentally deranged (quite believable) and that everything she'd said was a distortion of the truth? Did that mean he wasn't joining with Danila the bitch-witch?

Grace couldn't let go of the hurt long enough to believe that. But why else send her a message, if not to communicate something? It was none of her business if he was teaching or not. Pat had said the message was for her, not gossip, letting her know that he wasn't around and why.

There was no help for it. She'd have to talk to Elvira, confide in Elena and then sort herself out emotionally afterward. Unfortunately, her mother and Elena were out when she arrived home.

Grace paced around the house, full of nervous tension. That wasn't getting her anywhere so she went into the kitchen and decided to cook dinner. She'd completely forgotten about the Mexican feast she was going to make. She'd do something better. She flicked through the pages of her favorite recipe book and checked she had the necessary ingredients. Then she flicked on some music and sank into her food preparation, peeling small onions, chopping bacon and chuck steak, and sautéing the meat in olive oil and garlic. The aroma filled the room and Grace inhaled, closing her eyes. It seemed like an age since she'd last cooked from the heart. She put the meat on to simmer with some thyme and stock, then she started on the bread. She was a little late for the bread so she had to use magic to help it along. The butter was left over from her class and she stole a taste with some cheese on a cracker.

A smile broke out on her face. The butter was full of joy. Quite an intense spell because she'd had to imbue it several times during her demonstration. She laughed so hard as she buttered another cracker, and nearly choked. Hilarious. She was already full of happiness; any more butter and she'd burst.

There were some Kipfler potatoes handy so she decided to slice and bake them. With that all sorted, she still had the creative urge. Checking the cupboards and the refrigerator again, she decided a fruit crumble was just what she needed so she set herself to peeling, stopping to add mushrooms and wine to her beefy concoction.

By the time the others came home, Grace had

cooked up a feast. Her mother's eyes widened and then she smiled, giving a small, knowing nod.

'Feeling better, are we?'

Grace grinned. 'Better is a relative term. Let's just say that my earth mother came back with a bang and I had an overwhelming need to cook. You are hungry, aren't you?'

Elvira's grin grew wider. She headed down the hall. 'I'll just wash up and then set the table.'

Elena breathed deeply and then inhaled. 'My god. I think I'm in heaven. What is that heavenly smell?'

'Actually, it is the goddess you should be thanking and it's Beef Bourguignon with fresh-baked bread, asparagus with fresh hollandaise sauce, baked Kipfler potatoes, and a pear and apple crumble for dessert. But you'll have to pop up the road for double cream.'

Elena licked her lips. 'Right then. I'm off to get cream. I don't know what's gotten into you but I like it.' Elena picked up her handbag and darted away.

The front door shut, then items flew off from the table, the flower arrangement repositioned to the coffee table, the unopened mail to its holder by the door. Then the dresser trembled as plates shot off the shelves to glide gently onto the table-top and cutlery dueled across the room. Grace smiled. Her mother certainly had style.

Grace added her own touch, opening the back door to pick a single rose for the table. Her mother signaled that she was almost ready. Grace hailed Elena, who said she was on her way back. It was time to serve up.

Back in the kitchen, she ladled the Beef Bourguignon into a ceramic serving dish and the potatoes on a side dish. She popped the ingredients in the pot for the hollandaise and carefully monitored the steaming of the asparagus. Her mother took the bread to the table. When she came back for the beef, she saw the small dish of butter. 'Is that homemade?'

'Sure is. I taught my class today. Don't overdo it though. It is full of joy.'

Elvira laughed. 'I'm already full of joy, seeing you like this—so full of love and happiness in life itself. You have a wonderful gift.' She came over and kissed Grace's forehead. 'I'm blessed to have you in my life.'

Elena walked in. Elvira wiped her eyes. 'You are both so dear to me. Know that I love you with all my heart.'

'Here's the cream. You promised me food.'

'Go and sit down then. The asparagus is ready.'

'Wine?' Elena asked.

'Let's break out the bubbly I was keeping for a special occasion,' Elvira suggested.

'Let's not,' Grace said. 'I've already opened the red and we're eating red meat. Let's save the bubbly for something important.' She paused. 'Didn't we drink all the bubbly?'

'I bought more for another special occasion.' Her mother winked and Grace shook her head.

Elvira went into the kitchen to fetch the wine and Elena the glasses. Grace put the dish with the asparagus on the table, inhaling the butter smell of the hollandaise sauce and stopped to admire how prettily it was all set out.

Her mother poured wine, then took her seat. Elena lifted her glass. 'To Grace, the most important person in our lives. We love you.'

Grace lifted her glass. 'I love you back.'

Declan pushed out of the French doors and inhaled the mountain air. The private hospice was very picturesque, combining old-world charm and nature. A large, rambling weatherboard house, it was set within an acre of garden with bush surrounds. Birdcalls and the fragrance of wisteria and jasmine filled the air. At any other time, he would have found such a setting soothing. Now it reminded him that he'd been here for more than two weeks and he'd had enough.

He chewed his lip, restlessness creeping up his legs and into his spine. The urge to move was overpowering. His mother wasn't any better; the healer witch, Beatrice, hadn't been able to do much to cure his mother. He'd just walked out on a conversation where traditional human methods were being discussed and consideration given to them being beneficial. It wasn't that he didn't trust human methods—drugs, shock therapy and counseling—it was more to do with his mother.

If he thought objectively about her, the traits that had led to this meltdown had always been a part of Delores. They'd protected her, he and his father, and her family before that. In essence, his mother was flawed. Whether she'd been born that way, or was made that way by life, he didn't truly know. He doubted she could be cured, but with time she would return to the person she was, more functional but still as flawed. That he had let his mother hurt Grace wounded him deeply. He had to decide who came first in his life. It was a hard choice but one he had to make.

With clenched fists, he began to pace the garden, moving from sunlight to shade that made his sight flicker. What if he was flawed like her? He examined himself and could not see the signs. He needed an objective opinion. It was not without embarrassment that he recollected the stand-up row he'd had with Elvira. He hated what she'd said but he couldn't ignore the truth. No family was perfect, least of all his. Had Elvira's brother triggered these traits in his mother? Maybe, but they had been there below the surface.

In the late hours, his father and he had shared a few beers and talked. It all tumbled out, the life his father had lived with a woman he was bound to through duty and not love. It wasn't that his father had no fondness for his mother; it was more about choice. His father was seeing his own life through the spectrum of Declan's desires. Declan sensed that he would be willing to let Declan do as he pleased and damn the consequences. He was willing to give his blessing to Declan's freedom, a freedom he'd never had.

His mother, though? That would never happen. He'd have to accept that. She was unhinged now, and him not joining with Danila wasn't going to change that. Thoughts of Grace arose, her light spirit, her infectious laugh, her beautiful body and her joy in sex.

If he had to settle down, Grace would have been the right choice. Except it wasn't what he wanted. He just wanted to run from his life right then. His mother's and other people's expectations were crowding him until he thought he would drown.

His father called to him. It was his turn to sit with his mother. He did his duty, but the need to run free grew in him. He had to get away. Had to ride his bike and taste the wind. He wanted that endless road in front of him, the future a mystery to be discovered.

His father patted his shoulder as Declan entered the room. His father looked haggard and as soon as Declan sat down he knew why. His mother was in a state, eyes wide, mouth moving, words falling out in random order. In an effort to calm her, Declan took her hand and squeezed it. He talked to her softly about the weather, the trees and the house, which had been converted to a hospice. Incense burned in the room. It worked to calm him but did nothing for his mother. Beatrice came in.

'Your father asked me to come in to see what I could do.' The healer placed her hands on each side of his mother's head, her brows furrowing in concentration. 'There's something there. Some thread of something that I can't unravel. It's not a hex but it's something foreign.' She spoke quietly, more to herself with her eyes closed. Declan studied his boots and then looked up when he heard his name called.

'I'm sorry.'

'We need someone stronger than me. It's not something I can deal with. It's not just healing. A special talent is required.'

'Who do you recommend?'

'Well, the witch I have in mind is not a healer, but she is a very strong witch. I think her talent maybe useful. I was thinking of Grace Riordon.'

Declan stood up so fast his chair fell over. 'What? You must be out of your mind. My mother hates her, hates the whole family.'

'What about her mother, Elvira?'

Declan shook his head and bent to correct his chair. 'If it was up to me, I'd say yes in an instant. But I worry that we could make her worse by bringing them here.'

'Then we can try more calming potions, more rest, but her essential illness grows.' Beatrice worked on his mother, made her drink one of her potions. It made him angry that it was the best the older witch could do. It made him even angrier that she'd suggested Grace or her mother as witches who could help her.

He'd been away for many years, but nothing he'd heard or experienced himself would lead him to believe that Grace could help. Her ability with spirit, perhaps? Was there something wrong with his mother's spirit? Grace was very talented; who knew what she was capable of? After what she had suffered, he doubted Grace would even agree to help. He shook his head. Of course she would agree. Her generosity of spirit wouldn't allow her to do anything short of her best.

Declan dozed while he sat by his sleeping mother. His father came in and tapped him on the shoulder. 'You can take a break now.'

Declan yawned. 'Dad. I was speaking to Beatrice. I'm going to ask Grace or her mother to come and help.'

His father's eyes widened. 'You can't be serious.'

'I'm deadly serious. Beatrice can do nothing more. We can't live our lives like this. She can't live like this. We have to try it.'

His father shook his head. 'Her hatred of them is so strong.'

'Dad. I'm not going to sit here until she dies and do nothing. I'm not going to waste my life trying not to upset her because I want to follow my own path. Nor should you. You deserve a whole life. I'm going to ask them to come. Okay?'

His father wiped his hand across his forehead. 'If you think it's worth a try. It's better than the mental hospital and drugs.'

Declan slapped his dad on the back. 'I'll be back tomorrow. I doubt if I can get Grace to come before then.'

His father took the seat by the bed and lowered his head into his hands. Exhaustion and misery floated off him. Declan had to act for his mother's sake, and for his father's.

'Right. I'm off. I'll fetch Elvira and Grace and let's hope they can help.'

His father's red-rimmed eyes studied his face. 'They won't come. Too much bad blood. Delores has been wretched to Grace and was near feuding with Elvira before we left all those years ago.'

'Grace won't bear a grudge. I know it. Elvira might need convincing but if she's Grace's mother then I reckon they have that in common. Good, kind hearts. They'll come.'

His father's head drooped.

'I'll be back as fast as I can.'

It had been more than two weeks since her run in with Delores at the joining celebration. Other than that message, which was like an oasis in her life, she'd heard nothing from Declan. Grace had tried not thinking about him or about their lovemaking. Then she'd tried thinking of him and their lovemaking. It didn't make a difference, as she couldn't get Declan Mallory out of her mind.

A few days later, taking a moment's reprieve from the busy flow of her life, between school and home, Grace sipped her coffee and sat back in the booth seat of one of her favorite cafés in Balmain. Pedestrians rushed by on the street, hurrying to work, to the grocer, to school. It was a marvelous feeling, letting the world swim around her while she floated, undisturbed in a café, sipping a long black. A gem of contentment glowed inside her. There'd been no further word from Declan and that was okay. She was okay.

She hadn't decided what her feelings were yet. Either she was seriously in lust with him, and given Declan was an extraordinarily handsome well-built man, and fabulous, energetic and considerate in bed, that wasn't surprising. Most other witches were in lust with Declan and they didn't have her excuse. Or she was seriously in love with him. That was a tad scarier, given their shared history and the most recent events. Being in love for Grace meant joining. She could see no alternative end. If she loved, she gave of herself, her body and her life. She wanted children, and children with Declan? For goddess' sake, that would be awesome. What she did know was that she wasn't angry with him anymore and as she took another sip, she thought, she wasn't feeling hurt either.

Shaking herself, it dawned on her that she'd been staring into space. Not a good look. Tugging her magazines closer, she started flicking pages. The cooking magazine displayed tantalizing dishes and as she perused them, some caught her interest. Grace took out her notebook to jot some ideas down and became absorbed in what she was doing. A few minutes later a shadow fell over her. She'd been so lost in the pages of recipes that she hadn't detected the vibration of one of the folk approaching.

Lifting her head, she sat back in her seat and gasped. 'Danila?' she said, not quite able to mask her surprise. The bitch-witch was dressed in a tight black skirt and a low cut über-pink top. Grace managed a smile as best she could under the circumstances. She was sure she looked like a viper ready to strike, so she added more teeth to her smile and thought of something funny—like relating this scene to Elena over a few glasses of wine.

Danila fake-smiled at her and dropped her handbag on the floor. Grace sat speechless as Danila then smirked, flicked her blonde hair back over her shoulder and drew out a seat.

'Mind if I join?'

Grace froze, then quickly recovering, she said, 'Sure. Go ahead.' Her voice stuck in her throat like two-day-old porridge. *Why couldn't she speak in proper sentences? Like, get out of my face you shallow bitch-witch.*

Danila lifted a commanding finger, summoning the waiter while managing to look down her nose. 'I'll have a large soy chai latte please. And make it hot. I can't stand lukewarm drinks.'

The waited nodded and took in an eyeful of Danila's breasts, on display in her low-cut top.

Grace closed her magazine and tucked her notebook into her handbag. She took another sip of coffee and waited patiently. She wasn't making small-talk unless forced.

Danila leaned over the table and did a little slide with her fingers in front of Grace's face to get her attention 'So you've heard the news, I suppose. About the Dec and me?'

'The deck?'

'Declan Mallory and I are going to be joined.'

Grace did her best to keep her face composed. This was not what she was expecting to hear. 'Wow. Congratulations.'

'It's so fab.'

'Yes, I'm sure it is.'

Danila preened some more, flicking her gaze around the room to see who was admiring her and then batting her eyelids when she made eye contact with some random guy. Grace's stomach churned and bile rose in her throat. She wanted to puke. Actually she wanted to puke all over Danila. That brought an evil grin to her face. That would be so cool.

'His mother loves me. She was over the moon to see me naked in his arms in their backyard.'

Grace let mischief get the better of her. 'I'm sure. So is he good in bed?'

Danila's eyes looked up and then she locked gazes with Grace. 'Sure is.'

Grace smiled nastily and waited for an elaboration. When none came, she came in with a dart of her own. 'I heard he was rather under-endowed.' Grace wiggled her little finger. It was a mean thing to say but it was better than hexing the other woman, which she was sorely tempted to do, even though it was extremely bad mannered and her mother and the coven wouldn't approve.

Danila's mouth dropped open and then closed. She screwed up her face as she composed a reply. 'What a terrible rumor. He's just right for a big man. A comfortable fit.'

Grace leaned in closer, suspecting the lie but not able to read Danila. A stupid bitch-witch she might be, but she kept all her shallow thoughts locked up tight in her empty head.

Grace knew in her bones that Grace was lying. She couldn't have encountered Declan's appendage and been so blasé about it. He was extraordinary and in no way a comfortable fit. Besides, he was a wonderful lover and if Danila had banged him properly, she'd be grinning from ear to ear and boasting her head off. If she had done that, then Grace would've hexed her good and proper, boils on her face, hair falling out, tongue turning black—that type of thing. Of course it was only a thought, but she couldn't help imagining it and grinning at the same time.

'I'm sure you'll find him a satisfactory mate. He intends to live with his parents and have them help with any children.' Two could play at this game, Grace thought as she rubbed her chin. 'They want him to have…' Grace struggled to find a number. '… seven kids. One a year, preferably a couple of sets of twins so they can fill their home up with love and the sound of babies gurgling.'

A touch of guilt did wend its way into Grace's heart when she saw Danila's face turn grey. Her chai latte arrived and her eyes centered on it. It looked like it was her turn to throw up. A small tickling sense of guilt nagged Grace. Luckily it disappeared in a flash.

The way Declan's parents behaved added truth to her words. Grace was about to relent, admitting to teasing her, until Danila picked up her latte, took a sip and then looked down her nose at her. 'At least I'll have a mate, and children. I feel sorry for you, Grace. Such a boring life, boring looks, boring talents.' She leaned across the table and spun the magazine around. 'Cooking meals for your mother until she dies. And your sappy half-witch cousin making clothes for a living. How interesting and exciting.'

Grace's mouth dropped open. Danila downed the rest of her chai. *May it burn her evil throat.* She waltzed out, waving to the waiter and leaving Grace to pay for her drink. That tears it, thought Grace. With a quick and subtle twist of her magic, she dissolved the thread in the seam at the back of Danila's tight skirt so that it started to split. A happy glimpse of her underwear was a welcome sight before she stepped out of view. *That will teach her.*

After a few minutes digesting what had happened, Grace was less inclined to feel guilty. Obviously Danila hadn't heard any gossip concerning Declan's adventures between the sheets with Grace, yet how cruel was Danila? It hurt so much. Danila and Grace had used to play together when they were young, until Grace had raised Fel from the dead. Hadn't anything they'd been to each other survived? Was it all about competition and looks and one-upmanship?

At that moment, Grace was glad she had been shunned all these years. She was happy with the person she'd become. Maybe she would've turned out like Danila or some of the other more obnoxious bitch-witches. They weren't all bad, she knew that, but for some reason they ended up in her face, giving her a hard time.

Her eyes passed over the cake display and she thought a little pick-me-up worthwhile. No point in returning home full of negative vibes her mother would pick up and then interrogate her about. 'A salted-caramel macaron, thank you. And another long black, Roma blend.'

The waiter gave her a wink and Grace smiled, tucking her hair behind her ears. The waiter was

Italian and with Grace's olive skin and dark eyes and hair, she supposed she could pass for one too.

Her macaron arrived along with a fresh coffee. She was contemplating them and inhaling their aroma when Elena plonked herself down. 'Hi. I thought I might find you here.'

'Elena, how nice to see you. What are you wearing?'

She tugged on the material of her blouse. 'Do you like it?'

It was a peasant blouse, embroidered around the neckline. 'Did you make it?'

'Yes.' Elena frowned. 'A bit too…'

'It's fine if you were a gypsy, I guess. You sew really well though.' She peered closer at the stitching. 'Neatly done.'

Elena ordered a café latte. 'I just spoke to Danila, bitch face.'

'Really?'

'Yes, she's really down on you. How come you said Declan had a little…' She wiggled her pinky. 'I mean you never mentioned—' She screwed up her face. 'Now that I think of all the noise you made while you were at it, I don't believe that.'

Grace bit into her macaron to stop herself from smirking.

Elena squared her shoulders and tried to use her talent to read Grace. When that didn't work, she thought about it. 'I think I get it. You said it to get back at her, didn't you?'

Grace swallowed another mouthful of macaron. 'She intimated to me that she'd been sexually active with Declan, prior to their pending "joining". I thought I'd test that theory.'

'She was dead lying to you, wasn't she?'

Grace nodded before taking a sip of her coffee. 'I

don't feel bad at all, although Mother wouldn't approve. She said some pretty horrible things to me before she left.'

'That cow! As if you didn't have enough on your plate. You should never have let her have your Cinderella Barbie when you were kids. It melted her brain or something.'

Grace burst out laughing. 'I love you, Elena. Thank you for being in my life.' She leaned closer and told her what she'd done to Danila's skirt. Elena guffawed loudly, then snuck the last piece of Grace's macaron into her mouth.

'You go too far,' Grace said, mock indignantly.

'That was yum. Can we buy some to take home for dessert?'

'We sure can.' Grace finished the last of her coffee while Elena finished hers. They left the café arm in arm, a paper bag full of macarons of various flavors in Grace's bag.

CHAPTER EIGHT

'What's that?' Elena asked as they walked up the drive. Grace frowned at the motorbike parked there and stood stockstill, her shopping bags dropping to the ground. Elena ducked down to scoop them up. 'I'm guessing that means Declan is here.'

Grace's stomach churned, the coffee she'd drunk turning to acid. Her legs shook a little. She wasn't expecting to see him and was quite reluctant to. What if he had heard about the 'under-endowed' comment? She swallowed. 'Elena, give me my bags back.'

Elena passed them to her. 'Are you sure? You look very pale.'

'I'm fine. Like a sinking boat is fine during a cyclone.'

Elena made an *O* of surprise with her lips. Grace didn't move forward until her mother hailed her and told her not to keep dallying in the driveway in full view of their guest.

'Drat.'

She told Elena what her mother had said. 'Damn!'

'I couldn't have said it better.' Better composed,

Grace hoisted her shopping bags and followed Elena into the house.

'Here let me put these in your room,' Elena said, taking her shopping and ducking down the hallway.'

'Hello. I wasn't expecting to see you.'

Declan stood up from the sofa. He and Elvira had been in deep discussion, if the vibes in the room were anything to go on. The curtains were open, letting in the light and providing a full view of the driveway. She had been observed.

Her mother heaved herself off the sofa. 'I'll leave you two to talk. I've got some things to prepare and messages to send to the rest of the council.'

'Mother?'

'We'll talk later, dearest.' Elvira walked out of the room without a backward glance. Grace turned to Declan, a question on her lips.

Declan picked up her hand and squeezed it. 'It's good to see you again, Grace.'

'Thank you. Look, about the last time we spoke—'

'Yes...look I'm sorry about that. My mother isn't well. The fact is I need your help—yours and your mother's.'

'My help? I don't think she'd approve.'

'Beatrice from the healing center said you might and we've got nothing else. She said there was something foreign affecting my mother's mind.'

Grace sat down on the sofa, thoroughly puzzled. 'Beatrice Standish, the healer, recommended me?' She shook her head. 'I didn't even realize she knew I existed. How would she know...why would she think...?' Grace looked at the doorway where her mother had wandered. Elvira had been holding out on her.

'Will you come? That's all I'm asking.'

'Of course, I'll come and I'll do what I can but I

fear I'll be relying on my mother and Beatrice because I have no idea how I can help. Seeing your mother dislikes me so much, I really doubt that I can.'

He squeezed her hands gently and then leaned down to kiss on her on the forehead. 'Thank you. I knew you would. You mother is going to transport herself. I can take you on my bike. Is that okay?'

'Yes, sure. Give me a few minutes.'

Grace poked her head into Elena's room to let her know they were heading out. Elena frowned. 'You're going to help heal his mother? Do take care. I have a feeling that it's not going to be as straightforward as expected.'

'Is that your talent or general skepticizm?'

Elena shrugged. 'A bit of both. I just have a bad feeling'—She placed her hand on her stomach—'here.'

Grace had a similar feeling but she was so out of kilter with seeing Declan again, she couldn't see or sense clearly. 'That might be coming from me. You know I always transmit my anxiety to you. Or it could be because you're going to eat all the macarons by yourself and know you'll be sick after.'

Elena laughed and rubbed her stomach.

Fel jumped up on the bed and meowed eerily.

Hold on to that tom, Fel thought at her.

Grace frowned. She could take that two ways. *I'll try*, she thought back.

Elena rubbed its ghostly substance between the ears. Grace stared at the cat, expecting another sage or sarcastic comment, but it looked at her and meowed again, sending chills up Grace's spine.

'Did Fel talk to you again?' Elena asked.

Grace nodded.

'That's not fair. It's my cat. It should talk to me.'

'Hear that, Fel? Be nice to Elena.'

Fel flicked its tail and sauntered away.

'Snob,' Elena said to the departing cat.

Grace shrugged. 'I'd better go. I'll call you when I know something.'

Elena twisted her hair up into a knot. 'Okay. Takeaway pizza tonight!'

Grace shook her head. She wasn't even out of the house and Elena was indulging in junk food. She was incorrigible.

She received a parting hail from her mother as she brushed her teeth. 'See you there. Don't take long and be careful.'

Grace stewed over those words, seeking something underhanded. There was something very cloak and dagger about all this.

'I'm ready.' Declan wasn't in the living room as she came down the hall. She heard the revving of the motorbike. He was ready to roll. She marched outside and received a grin and a helmet. In no time they were off, back to the Blue Mountains where they'd spent their first night. *Mustn't think about that now. Particularly while you have your arms wrapped around all that man.*

Grace had time to think on the way out to the health center. Declan was troubled. It was clear from meeting him again and from holding him. He was pretty good at keeping a lid on his thoughts and feelings, so much wasn't leaking through. A sense of relief and hope flowed through him, knowing that she was coming to help. That was rather daunting, considering she'd not healed anyone before. She was good at sensing people, detecting if they'd been hexed, but surely Beatrice would have been able to pick that up and deal with it herself.

Grace took in the landscape whizzing past—the rows upon rows of houses and the grey blue of the mountains growing larger the further they sped down the Great Western Highway.

When she climbed off the bike, she was a bit stiff. Her legs were not very cooperative so she stomped on the spot and massaged her lower back. Declan put the gear away in the panniers. The sun was setting and the view to the city and across the large tranche of bush took on a peachy hue. It was a majestic spot. A little too prone to bushfires for Grace's liking, but the mountains had a fantastic vibe, as if goddess and earth met there.

They walked around the path, through neatly tended gardens to the front door. To a casual observer it was a large, historic house. To the coven, it was a place of healing.

'You really should learn to transport yourself, my dear.' Elvira gave her a kiss on her cheek. An older woman with greying hair tied up in a bun and wearing a flowing dress in brown cottage print stood behind her.

'This is Beatrice. You probably don't remember her very well.'

She had a flash of insight and Grace remembered childhood images of this woman touching her. She recalled her smile and light spirit. 'I don't remember you well, but I do have some vague recollections from when I was a child.'

Beatrice smiled, revealing startling, white straight teeth. 'You have grown up to be so beautiful. You are full of light and love.' She touched a finger to Grace's cheek. 'You have your father's dark complexion, but I see Elvira in you too. You have her sparkling eyes, and probably a great deal of her wit too.'

'Thank you for the compliments. I'm at a bit of a loss to know how I can help.'

Beatrice lowered her gaze. 'Perhaps we can talk in

private.' Grace stiffened as Declan sucked in a surprised breath at the attempt to exclude him.

'Perhaps somewhere where we can all sit down comfortably?' She turned to include Declan.

'I'll be with you in a moment,' he said. 'I have to pop in and see my mother and let my father know you are here. He may want to listen in on your discussions.'

Beatrice and Elvira shared a look. 'Of course, come into the lounge. There's no one else about. I suppose I should organize food too. It will be a long night.' Beatrice closed her eyes, and Grace felt a slight tingle as the older witch sent a message to someone, probably the kitchen staff.

The lounge room had a large leather lounge suite with enough space to seat ten people. The curtains were still parted, the dark velvet invoking the Victorian era. Photos graced the mantelpiece and one wall was stacked with bookshelves. Grace sighed as she sank into her seat. She wanted one of these leather couches when she settled in her own place.

A young witch came in bearing a tray. 'Thank you, Jessie.' Beatrice turned to Elvira. 'My granddaughter.'

Elvira nodded and smiled as the girl walked away. Beatrice passed around tea in dainty cups. Grace took hers. While she didn't pry into all her mother's interactions, she'd never heard her speak of this particular old healer witch and as far as Grace knew, Beatrice hadn't come to the house, not in recent years. Yet, there was an obvious connection between them, a fond friendship.

'Now, about Delores.'

Declan came in at that moment. Elvira indicated a seat. 'We were just starting. Tea?'

Declan waved the tea away. Grace detected his increased anxiety. He must be extremely stressed for her to detect it from where she sat.

'Is your father joining us?' Beatrice asked.

Declan shook his head. 'He is staying with my mother for a bit longer.'

'Right then,' Beatrice said. She took a long drink of her tea and set the cup aside, then she folded her hands across her lap and looked at them in turn. She cleared her throat. 'I believe that Delores is suffering from an infestation.'

'Infestation?' Grace blurted.

Elvira lifted her hand, signaling for quiet.

'I think it's a fragment of er…how do I say this…a spirit.'

Declan sat up straighter. 'You're talking possession.'

Beatrice shrugged. 'Not quite a possession. At least, that's what I think. Something is troubling her, eating at her. It was hard to detect, to make certain, but I got a sense of something else there. Like the scent of bad meat.' She turned over her hands in a helpless gesture.

Elvira made eye contact with Grace and then inclined her head. Grace swirled her tongue around in her mouth while she considered what they were saying. 'You think I can connect or in some way detect this spirit fragment, if that's what it is?'

'Yes, darling. That's what Bea thinks.'

'And you?'

'I think you have the talent and the strength for this.'

Grace thought about the rules she'd been taught. She'd need permission but even then it skirted on outlawed. Declan picked up her hand. 'Please, Grace. Try.'

'I have your permission? I mean, I can't imagine your mother would or could give it to me.'

Declan nodded and squeezed her hand again. 'I've spoken to my father and he has given his permission for you to assist.' He lifted her hand and kissed her knuckles. 'Grace, I would love to have my mother whole. Please help her.'

Grace extracted her hand. 'I can only try. I hope the coven is cool with this because contacting dead things is not something they're keen on.'

'We are both here to watch over you, dear,' Elvira said. She stood up and turned to Declan. 'This may not work. Grace may not be able to help your mother. I am not being pessimistic, but I think you should be prepared. There is a risk of harm, if this fragment is too integrated into your mother.'

He nodded. 'I am. Beatrice said it was a chance only. The alternative is to have her locked up in a mental institution with no hope of recovery.'

'Then let's do it,' Elvira said.

'This way,' Beatrice said as she got up and went to the door. 'Declan, it would be best if you took your father for a walk or something. Elvira will hail you if there is any news.

'But…'

'It's best this way. Believe me. We'll take good care of your mother.'

Declan frowned and shifted his gaze to Grace. He mouthed a *thank you* and turned to leave the room. Grace followed her mother and the healer. She had no idea what she was to do, but obviously her mother thought she did.

A hard light bathed the room in glare. Grace sheltered her eyes. 'Can you dim that a little?' The light lowered.

In the few weeks since Grace had seen Delores,

she'd grown thinner. Her hair was straggly, hanging down her shoulders, and her eyes were ringed in grey shadows. Meaningless words flowed past her lips. She was oblivious to her surroundings. Or was until Grace approached. Delores stiffened, then her feet banged against the mattress and her jaw clenched as breaths were sucked in with desperate heaves.

'Interesting,' Beatrice said.

Grace spared her a look. 'Frightening. Why is she doing that?'

The pair of them said nothing. 'It's me, isn't it?'

Her mother tilted her head to the side and shrugged.

Grace shut out Delores's reaction and drew closer, using her witch sense to peer inside her. A lot of bad emotions writhed there, caught in some kind of vortex that churned them, tying them together. Yet that wasn't what was making her ill.

Grace sent her gaze deeper and caught motion at the edge of her perception. Was that a snake? Or a worm? She wiggled between the swirls of hatred that curled around Delores's center. There she positioned herself, trying to blend in with the surroundings. It wasn't going to work, but waiting would give her time to acclimatize and also to act. There it was again. A fleeting presence. She almost detected it, identified it. Beatrice was right. It was foreign.

Elvira spoke to her, mind to mind. *Can you see it?*

Yes. Briefly. But it slips away and hides from me.

Grace stayed quiet in Delores's essence, waiting for that thing to return. Out of the blue, the attack came. It was like being smothered with a blanket of hate. Grace struggled at first, having underestimated its furtive nature. It tried to infiltrate her, then faltered. Elvira attacked it, ripping at it and trying to drain it. Next thing she knew, Grace found herself on the floor. Declan hovered over her.

'What?'

'You cried out. I heard you.' Declan helped her to stand. 'I was outside in the garden. You called to me. I'm sorry.' He ran his fingers through his hair and shrugged when the others gaped at him. 'I guess I shouldn't have done that.'

Elvira and Beatrice shared a look. 'No harm done,' Beatrice said.

'Thank you, Declan.' Her eyes sought her mother. 'Well?'

'I don't recognize him.'

'Him?'

'Why do I get the feeling that you're not telling me everything? You suspect a particular spirit fragment, don't you?'

Declan stroked her back and glared at the two older witches. 'You think it's Elroy, don't you?'

Beatrice made herself taller, shaking out her shoulders and straightening her spine. 'I entertained the possibility. Grace, what did you detect?'

'It's hard to say, exactly. It appears to be male. That is what I sensed from it. I get the sense that it was once one of the folk. It had a strong connection to Delores.'

'Try again, dear. This time I want you to touch it. We need to know more so you can extract it.'

'Extract it? Touch it? It near smothered me. It acted like I was the enemy, like it wanted me dead.'

The healer scratched her chin. 'Interesting.'

'Interesting? Is that what you call it? Downright freaky if you ask me.'

'We are here to protect you,' her mother said calmly. 'Go on, dear. I'm getting hungry.'

Grace snorted. 'Right. Hungry. I get it.'

Grace let her talent unfold, this time bringing her hands to Delores's head, not quite touching. She found this helped her focus. The presence was waiting for her this time, no longer hiding. It rose up and whacked her. Her knees buckled, and strong hands held her around the waist. Declan.

The contact with the fragment was more tangible this time. It definitely had a strong bond to Delores. There. It was discernible now. It was young, but its sense of identity was blurred. Grace had to be careful because she didn't want to bring it across to life, like she had the cat. She wanted to untangle it and send it packing. It aimed for her again and Grace drew in her senses, pulled back on her talent and sagged against Declan.

Her mother held some port to her mouth. Grace took a sip, letting the sweet spirit slide down her throat. She took some more. Declan sat her on the floor, crouching beside her. She looked up and all three were waiting expectantly.

'It's a spirit. A young, male spirit.'

'The brother?' Elvira ventured.

'Could be,' Beatrice said, her gaze on Delores. 'His spirit was not exiled like Elroy's, so it could be that the way he died prevented him from departing.'

Elvira bit her bottom lip, her blue eyes sparkling. 'Grace, if it's Saul, then he died suddenly and in horrible circumstances. It is possible that he clung to his sister, still clings to her. She found him, was there when he died. If his spirit lingered, he could have latched onto her. It would explain how she reacts to you. Although you have your father's coloring you do take after my side in looks and you have that connection to the dead.'

'I don't have a connection to the dead. I just have

difficulty telling who is alive and who is dead…sometimes.'

'What now, then?' Declan asked. 'Can you free her from this fragment?'

Grace didn't know how to answer so she kept her mouth shut. Beatrice rubbed her chin, deep in thought. Grace cocked her eyebrow at her mother, who shrugged. That was a surprise. Her mother, stumped.

'No point in lingering here. I have some research to do. You lot may as well eat while I come up with something.' The healer headed out of the room and then turned around suddenly causing them all to stop in their tracks. With a gesture at Grace and Declan she said, 'No indulging in sex, you two. Grace, you need to be clear of mind and body for this next step.'

Grace's cheeks burned. 'We were…we aren't…' She turned to Declan for some help. He shrugged. *What did that mean?* Grace thought to herself.

Whatever had happened to Declan that day, it didn't affect his appetite. He had two large plates of roast beef with all the trimmings and was getting ready to dig into a big bowl of creamed rice. He saw Grace's expression and grinned at her.

'I've hardly eaten in days. Now that you're here and there's a possibility that something can be done, my spirit has lifted and my appetite has returned.' Beatrice's granddaughter came in to clear off the plates. 'May I have another serving?' He lifted his shoulders. 'It's for my father. He's resting for a while but he'll be hungry when he wakes.'

'I have a meal prepared for him, Battle Master Mallory. Just send me a hail when he's ready.'

Grace studied the young woman. Inviting an eligible warlock to hail you was rather forward, or did she think so because she was jealous? She shook her head.

'What?' Declan was wide-eyed as he waited for a response.

'Nothing.'

'It wasn't nothing. You shook your head.' He narrowed his eyelids.

'I was distracted, thinking about what happens next. That's all.' Her cheeks must be glowing.

A slight smile tugged at Declan's cheek. 'You really are a bad liar. But, if you aren't going to tell me now, you will tell me later, when there's less going on. Deal?'

'Sure thing.' She agreed but hoped the incident would be forgotten. It hadn't escaped her notice that he was rather cool with her. Yes, he had stuff going down with his family, but he treated her as a friend, not as a lover. Was this what Elvira was worried about, that Declan was going to break her heart? No guesswork or talent was needed to predict that.

They were sitting around drinking coffee when Beatrice came in. 'I've been studying up on this phenomenon. It's not quite a possession, so the normal type of exorcism and exiling ritual won't work. It is a fragment of her brother that reached out to her when he died. They were very close and she grieved hard. Both those things combined have worked together to build on this fragment, which in the beginning was barely more than a memory. Now it has substance and given Delores's decline, I'm thinking the fragment is draining her.'

'Draining her, why?' Grace asked.

'Because it's been fed all these years by Delores's grief and her memories and her love. It now thinks it is her brother, but it's not. It's a fragment. Grace, you are going to have to lure it out of her. It will come to you if it thinks you'll give it life.'

Grace shook her head. 'I can't do that. I don't want to be punished again.'

'It won't survive outside Delores. It's only a fragment and has no coherence. When you draw it out, Elvira and I will perform the exiling ritual. Declan, you will have to help. Do you know the steps?'

He nodded decisively. 'Well then, if you are ready, then let's do it.'

Grace went to the kitchen to thank the cook. Maddie was pleased to be thanked. Grace didn't consider it stalling when she went to the bathroom to relieve herself, wash her face and breathe deeply for ten minutes before emerging. She didn't know Beatrice well. What if something went wrong? Could Declan do anything? He was a battle mage, but did that include fighting intangible beings?

Standing with her hand on the doorknob she tried to talk herself up, even though it was weird to be going against the teachings of the last ten years. A knock on the door made her jump. 'Grace?'

She opened the door. 'Sorry.'

Declan's frown showed concern. 'Will you be all right, Grace?'

She rubbed her hands together. 'Sure. Lead on.'

He turned around and she forced herself to follow. She wasn't about let him know she was afraid, not when so much was resting on the outcome.

Another witch was in the room with Beatrice and Elvira when Grace and Declan entered. 'This is Angie. She is here to reinforce the circle. Declan you stand there. Grace you stand at the head of Delores and we'll encircle you,' Beatrice said. Candles burned in niches around the room and the strong scent of myrrh wafted around them. 'Anytime you're ready, Grace.'

They joined hands with eyes closed. Grace looked down at Delores who still mumbled. *Goddess protect me*, Grace prayed, and dove in. The fragment was stronger than previously and had more substance. She sent her senses around the edges and saw where it was anchored to Delores, draining her of her life energy. That was a bit easier to deal with because she could see where to make the cut.

So you want to live, do you? Come with me then. Come on.

The fragment understood her and rushed at her. At first, Grace suffocated under the weight of its presence. She fell back figuratively, drawing the fragment with her. At the same time she lashed out, severing its connection with Delores, who jerked under her hands. The gasps from the circle confirmed she had drawn it out and they could see it.

To be sure, she sent her senses back into Delores while the chant rose up around her. Delores was very weak. Grace did what she could to boost her breathing and giving a little of her own essence to help her recover. When she was stable, Grace withdrew her talent and opened her eyes. She had to stay very still in case she broke the circle.

The fragment appeared like a stain, a grey smudge, and it fought the ritual to exile it. Grace put up a barrier to block it coming into her and then quickly extended it to Delores. Declan's mother was weak and the fragment was likely to seek refuge there once again. As she was not part of the circle there was nothing she could do to help them. Her mother's power flared. Grace cast her gaze sideways and saw Declan's power, a burning greenish gold, strike with force. The fragment was weakening. Beatrice's power was steady and strong and Grace could see her unraveling the fragment, pulling a small thread so that it weakened slowly without actually detecting how.

Delores was coming around. Grace leaned over and whispered to her while stroking her forehead. 'It's all right now. You'll get better soon.' Delores sighed and drifted off to sleep, breathing with a rhythm normal, her life force growing stronger.

Beatrice spoke out, her eyes unfocussed. 'Declan. I want you to thrust into the very centre of it when I say now.'

'Yes.'

The chanting rose in pitch. Sweat was pouring off Angie and Elvira's power had lessened. The healer gave a mental heave. 'Now!'

The words of exile filled the room as Declan attacked, and the fragment dissipated and was no more.

Beatrice said the words to end the circle and they let go of each other's hands. Grace backed away as Declan surged forward. He brushed the hair from his mother's face. 'Mom?'

Delores opened her eyes and then smiled. 'Declan?'

Beatrice left the room and returned very quickly with Mr Mallory in tow. He stood there, gaping at the scene in front of him. 'Delores?'

'I was in a dark place.' Delores spoke in a feeble voice.

He rushed forward and grabbed her hand. 'I know. I know.'

Grace backed away so she could sidle to the door unnoticed. Mr Mallory turned to her. 'Thank you. Thank you for what you have done.'

Grace blushed and then ran out of the room, suddenly overcome with emotion. Her mother came after her and held her tight. 'You did well, dear. You did brilliantly. You saved that poor woman's life.'

'Oh Mom, I was so scared.'

'I know, but you're brave. You didn't let your fear rule you. Now, maybe this coven will let you be the witch you were meant to be.'

She held Grace's face between her hands and wiped the tears with her thumbs. 'I'm going to head back. You can get a ride with Declan in the morning. Okay?'

Grace nodded. 'Okay, sure.'

Her mother dematerialized. 'Neat skill that,' she said to the air. She didn't really want to hang around, but it was a bit late to catch a train.

Beatrice bustled in. 'There you are. I have a room for you to rest in. I suspect you are very tired after all that. We don't want you swooning anytime soon. Come along. I'll show you. The Mallorys will be needing some time together, I suspect.'

Grace cast a look over her shoulder at the door to Delores's room. She didn't send her talent in to see what was going on. That was private. She recalled the look Mr Mallory had given her. The absence of hate surprised her. When she thought about it a bit more, as she followed Beatrice to the room set aside for her, she liked not being hated.

The room had a big brass bed, draped in lace. The furniture was carved oak and the curtain dark velvet. A rag rug kept her feet off the polished floorboards. 'It's lovely. Thank you.'

'There's a shower and toilet through those doors there and the French windows open onto the garden. Enjoy.' The healer kissed her on the cheek. 'I always knew you'd grow up into a very special witch.'

Grace blinked. 'You did? Tell me, in what circumstances did we meet?'

Beatrice fiddled with her bun. 'Well, that was after the incident with the cat. The council asked me to examine you for…well…unsavory influences.'

'I see, and you didn't find any?'

'No, dear, just strength and talent. Your spirit has always been light.'

'Thank you. Good night, Beatrice.'

'Good night, dear. Only get up when you want to. There will be food ready at any time. Take your ease.'

Grace stripped off and headed to the shower. She sniffed her clothes and pulled a face. She'd worked up quite a sweat during the ritual. She spell-cleaned her clothes and hung them up and then stepped into the shower. The hot water caressed her body as she let go of all the emotion she'd experienced that day. Thinking about what she'd done, it was as if it was the first time in her life that she'd done something of real value for her community. She examined her feelings, and it wasn't because Declan had asked her. She'd been able to put her love for him aside and deal with the request.

Love? Did she really believe it was love? Not the childhood love she'd cherished for him, but adult love? She put her face into the hot spray, wetting her hair and opening her mouth so the water cleansed her throat too.

When she got out she discovered she hadn't packed pajamas, so it was naked to bed. It was heavenly to slip between the crisp white sheets. Yet even then, Grace found it hard to sleep. The excitement of being able to help his mother, the new experience of encountering a fragment and dealing with it were all occurrences that allowed her to grow as a witch. Then there was the proximity to Declan and not being able to tell whether he cared for her or not. Well, she knew he cared but she didn't know what he would risk for that.

Her heart thumped hard. Acknowledging the love did nothing for her situation. Declan was distracted and cold. He had no time to think about love right now, especially love to a woman his mother hated. Maybe now she wouldn't hate her as much as she had previously, but Grace could not picture a future where that would be.

Yet, having him near was enough to send her senses into a spin. She may have been scared, but now that the fear was gone, her thoughts could focus on more interesting things. Too bad she'd left Randy Roger at home. All that man so close and so far away.

Although she was tired she tossed and turned, only dozing occasionally. A few hours after she retired, there was a tentative hail from Declan.

Are you asleep? It was a thin thread of a query that if she had been asleep she would have missed it.

Yes, she replied back. *You?*

The vibration of his light laughter reached her. *Do you want company?*

I thought you'd never ask.

Grace had but a few moments to restore the bed-covers before Declan joined her. Already naked, he slid between the sheets and drew her close. Declan was in need of comfort. She held him, stroked him in an undemanding way while he cuddled against her, his mind quiet. Grace found it hard to have all that man so warm and close, but after a while she relaxed and drifted off to sleep, still wrapped in his arms. His stillness helped to quiet her mind.

It must have been an hour or so later that Declan came around to more interesting things. Grace woke to the hands exploring her back, cupping her buttocks and then sliding up to cradle her breasts. Lifting her head, she kissed him fully, letting him know that she was awake and willing. He responded with long, drawn-out kisses that left her whimpering for more. Yet, his mood was different, sombre. This wasn't about excitement and sex; it was about connection and comfort.

Grace took delight in touching him, running her fingers along his chest. With a groan, Declan lifted her so that she lay on top of him, which gave his hands free access. *I love to touch your skin, to have all of you surround me.*

His mind voice spoke intimately to her. She reached out, sending him a brainwave that would send him reeling. It was a little parcel filled with the sensations she was enveloped in, the sheer and utter bliss of having her skin on his, his heat radiating around her and his very impressive erection nestled between her thighs. Within a heartbeat, he'd flipped her over.

Grace. Oh, Grace. Do I really excite you that much?
Stay connected to me and find out.

Declan was ready and Grace was so ready he slid inside before she took a breath. The electrical buzz of excitement went straight to her brain. He took another experimental lunge and received an even more impressive burst of ecstasy from Grace.

That could get addictive. It's like being surrounded by endorphins. Exploding neurons.

My thoughts exactly. She smacked him lightly on the thigh. He'd stopped moving. *No time to smell the roses.*

The more they moved, the more open the connection between them became. Grace didn't mean to pry but she couldn't help but notice the dark mass of emotion that roiled like a thundercloud inside him.

He shielded her from it the best he could as their bodies moved, a slow grind that had Grace gasping for breath and Declan growling as he caught the feedback from her. Declan was heaven on this earth, she thought idly. *No wonder I love him so much.*

She was very close to climax now and Declan's ardor was dark and dangerous. Her orgasm hit her, fierce and fast. Then the flavor of his mind changed; he came, hard and drawn-out. While he held his weight, he didn't move from on top of her. Grace sensed that he'd fallen asleep. He was utterly exhausted.

After about fifteen minutes he rolled to the side, bringing her with him. Grace let down all her defenses and slept the sleep of the dead.

At the first whisper of dawn, grey light filtered into the room. The bed was empty.

CHAPTER NINE

It was still early when Declan hailed her and asked her to meet him in the garden. Why had he left her without waking her? She'd stayed abed wondering about it. The mass of confusion and pain she detected in him would be hard to negotiate. The business with his parents only made things worse. She chewed her lip, wondering if there was something else wrong. Was it her he didn't want to be around? She shook her head. They'd had a magical evening together. Melancholy, yet beautiful in the degree of closeness they shared. As she slipped outside in the crisp morning air, she was going to find out.

Declan stood under a tree. A small bench seat was situated nearby. Currawong calls echoed in the trees and the grey-green leaves of Eucalypts overshadowed the bright pinks, whites and mauves of the daisies blossoming in the cottage garden.

Declan's forehead was clouded with worry as he stood with his hands in the pockets of his black leather riding jacket, staring at the daises and scuffing the carefully manicured lawn. Her eyes dropped lower. Leather pants and his bad-ass boots. He was off for a ride somewhere. He had this air of travel, of leaving. Grace battened down the hatches on her emotions. The reason she woke up alone was becoming clear.

At the sound of her step, he looked up. A fleeting smile crossed his face, yet his dark eyes were somber.

'How is your mother this morning?' she asked by way of greeting.

He kissed her cheek and a smile lit up his eyes for a moment. 'Much better, thanks to you. Beatrice thinks she will be on the mend shortly. Last night, my father had the best sleep in a long time.' He took her hands in his and rubbed at the tips of her fingers idly, not looking her in the eye.

'That's good. Look, Declan. You may as well spill. What's troubling you? Why are you dressed like that this early?' She wanted to add, *why did you leave me alone in bed?*

He nodded once and then scooped her hair away from her face, cupping her chin. She looked him square in the eye.

'Grace, I'm leaving for a while. I have to get away for a bit.'

'How long?' she asked softly. It was hard work keeping her voice neutral. They'd shared a magical night together, had touched minds as well as bodies. How could he walk away from that?

He shrugged. 'I can't say. Things are sorting themselves out with my parents but I'm confused inside. Even if my mother is cured, I know there are expectations about me settling down. It's not just them; it's the coven. This has been building for a while. I have to just make a break, establish myself so that it's clear to everyone I'm my own man. That I call the shots in my life.'

'I didn't have any expectations about you settling

down.' *Only hopes and dreams that I dared not share with anyone.*

Their gazes locked. 'I know you've never put any expectations on me and I appreciate that more than you could know. But it's like there is pressure building up inside me. I feel like it's going to blow. I need time and space to sort it out before this confusion, this restlessness destroys me.'

Grace swallowed, bracing herself for what he was going to say next, bracing herself for the big goodbye.

'I want you to know that if I were going to join with someone, it would have been you.'

Grace did her best to keep her face neutral. Now wasn't the time to swoon or burst out wailing, even though he was ripping the very heart of out of her 'The light inside you fills me up. We go so well together in many ways.'

Grace chewed her bottom lip. How was she supposed to react to this I-almost-love-you-but-I-can't-settle-down speech? 'You gave me a good first time.' She smiled what she hoped was a convincing smile.

He chuckled lightly, yet was still overwhelmingly serious. 'Yes, that was amazing—every time with you is.'

Grace folded her arms in front of her. 'Look, Declan. You don't owe me any explanation. It's your life. You made no promises to me, not even hinting of anything more. I mean, anyone would think I was the last person on your list, given how much both your parents disliked me.' She didn't mean to sound waspish, but it was time to run somewhere. Hiding what she was feeling was taking a great deal of effort. There was no way she'd let him know of her heartbreak, her love.

His eyes widened. 'But I want to explain myself to you. I care for you deeply, Grace. We have a connection, a special connection. We always have done. I turned my back on you when you needed me that day nine years ago and now it looks like I'm doing it again.'

'That was different. You were a child. I was a child.'

'Yet I remember, Grace. How close we were. What we shared. What a rare thing it was.'

'You do?' Grace was surprised that he admitted it, their childhood touching of the minds. It was brief, intense, and she'd begun to think she'd imagined it.

'Of course I did. I've never had that with anyone else.'

'Me neither.'

'Last night too was the most intimate I have ever been. I know you care for me, Grace. At that moment when we touched our minds, you couldn't hide it. I know how you feel.'

Grace widened her eyes. Had she let that slip? Was he that perceptive?

'You love me.' He studied her face.

'I've always loved you,' she blurted out, hoping to lessen the damage a stray thought had caused. 'That's just how it is between you and me. It's part of the fabric of us. Yet, that doesn't mean I'm in love with you.'

With a nod, he lifted his hand and brushed the hair out of her face. 'You are very beautiful to me. I love your skin, your dark eyes and your hair. Most of all, I love your smile and your laugh.'

Grace studied his face, reached out with her witch sense and knew him to be speaking what he felt was truth. 'I will miss you while you are gone.'

He angled his head to assess her. 'You think I'm coming back?'

'I know you are. Someone has to rescue me from Randy Roger.'

He burst out laughing and hugged her to him. 'Oh, Grace. You really do fill my heart with such joy.' He kissed her forehead.

'I can't promise I'll be back. I have this urge to be free, to just drive and drive and not look back. These last few weeks seem like a thunderhead and I want to escape from it, from the negative emotion, the guilt, the sadness. It has been with me for a while now. Ever since we came back here. I thought it was the pressure I was under to do what my parents wanted. I thought maybe I was missing the UK and the potential to be the top battle mage in Europe. I thought I wanted to love. Then I thought I didn't want love.'

'Declan, you've been through a lot recently. It's been tough on you, changing countries, covens, and I agree there was amazing pressure on you. You forget I met a few of your stalkers.'

He chuckled some more and then drew her closer so that they embraced lightly. 'I'll think of you.'

Grace closed her eyes and hoped she wouldn't cry. She had to have faith that Declan would sort himself out. 'Are you leaving right now?' She stepped out of his hold, but still kept close.

'Yes. I need to. I have to get away.'

'Go on then. Take care of yourself.'

With a quick nod to her, he left the garden. A few minutes later she heard his bike start up, then the sound of him driving away reached her ears. With a heavy sigh, she slumped on the bench seat, listening but not really listening to the sound of insects buzzing past. If there was a Currawong doing its sing-song call nearby, she didn't hear it. A numbing nothingness floated inside her. Declan cared for her but didn't love her enough to make anything of it.

That was the negative view, she supposed. The posi-tive view was that he considered that if he had wanted to settle down it would have been with her. Well, that was as positive as she could make it. She let out a big sigh and sat back in the seat, then she frowned. 'I guess that means I'm catching the train back to Sydney. Excellent. That must be two addi-tional brooding hours I don't need. What joy!'

After saying her goodbyes, Grace made enquires of Beatrice's granddaughter, who offered her break-fast. Grace took some coffee and a fresh muffin and then left the hospice to walk up the hill to the Ka-toomba train station. She stood in the sunshine while she waited for the train. It was a long time arriving so she surreptitiously studied the other passengers. It wasn't often she used public transport. A young couple doted on a small boy in a stroller. An Asian teenager listened to music while playing with his phone. Two older women gossiped about another woman, a mutual friend she presumed, and a couple of lanky teenage boys lounged against the wall in gunmetal-grey T-shirts and played games on little handhelds.

Eventually, the train pulled up and Grace hoped to secure a seat by herself somewhere. Unfortunately, the train was reasonably full. She had a seat to herself but not a carriage. Then when the kept stopping at all the stations, she knew she was the slow train. Per-haps the study of teleporting was something she should aspire to. As her talents lay in a different area, she didn't fancy her chances. It was unlikely she'd ever transport herself anywhere, except maybe to the other side of death, and she really didn't want to do that.

Resting her head on the window, she watched un-seeing as houses, parks and trees rolled past before the train slowed for the next stop and then jerked when it started again. Declan must have been pretty distracted. It wasn't like him to forget he'd brought her to Katoomba and leave her there. It wouldn't be like him to forget such a detail. That thought comforted her a bit, because it proved in her mind just how upset and confused he was.

Declan drove, caressing the speed limit liberally as he joined the freeway north. The passing of miles helped him sort through things. It was awful being so confused, so conflicted. It was a new kind of torture. His parents would sort themselves out now. They had to because he wasn't going to be there for them. He didn't have to worry about them anymore. His choices were his own to make and his father had accepted that, although reluctantly. Making the break with them had been painful, but so liberating when the worst of the anguish was over. With his mother on the mend, his father was less clingy and more understanding of his need to be free.

But now that he was free to make a choice, he didn't know what he wanted. The wind was a hard wall that buffeted him. A B-double truck overtook him and cut in way too close. Declan braked. The truck had snuck up on him.

He checked his mirror and swung out. He upped his speed and overtook a line of sleek sedans. Now he was free and he'd said his goodbye, he couldn't get Grace out of his mind. She loved him; no matter what she said about 'being in love with him', he knew she was.

He was in love with her. That thought jolted him.

He overtook a pick up truck and a rusty green minivan and ducked back into the left lane.

He checked his mirror and overtook the semi-trailer ahead of him. It was going so fast, Declan went twenty miles over the speed limit before nudging back into the left lane. The road looked clear ahead of him.

What was he doing driving away from her? He should be driving toward her, toward the future he was so afraid of. Oh goddess, he'd left her stranded in Katoomba. What an ass he was. Yet, he knew she'd forgive him. She understood. They were kindred spirits.

Something changed within. Driving had helped clear his head and the temporary freedom allowed his worries to unravel. Clearing the air with his father had eased that tangled nest of emotions he'd been wrestling with. He could see clearer now. Life with Grace would be amazing. She gave him room to do what he must. Then he knew that joining with her was what he wanted. It was something he needed to do straight away. He drove a few more miles and the certainty grew. He had to get back to her. Had to.

He heard the blare of a horn. He checked his mirror. The semi-trailer he'd passed was bearing down on him. He looked at his speedometer and realized the semi's brakes must have failed. The horn blared again.

By the time they reached Penrith, Grace was searching for her phone. When she retrieved it from her handbag, it was out of charge. Great. She was too far to hail Elena. As she hadn't slept well she was rather fatigued. She must have dozed off because she was woken by a large body sitting next her. Startled, she gaped the carriage was nearly full. She sat up straight and moved her handbag so it sat on the side closest to the window. This train ride was as much of the human world as she wanted to experience for a while, seeing all she wanted to do was lock herself in her room and listen to music with lyrics about broken, bleeding and desperate hearts.

The window thumped her on the head, waking her suddenly. The train was pulling out from Strathfield and a completely new set of passengers now filled up the carriage. Rubbing her eyes, Grace tried to get with it. *Mother*. She sent a hail.

There was no response. *Mother!*

Grace chewed her bottom lip. What was her mother on about? She could hear her at this distance. It was still too far to raise Elena.

Grace checked the train map and decided it was best to get off at Redfern and catch a taxi. Then she thought maybe she should change trains to get off at Circular Quay and take the ferry.

By the time she reached Redfern, the decision was made. Her mother stood on the platform. Grace hadn't expected to be met. She swept onto the station as soon as the doors opened. The smile on her lips fled. 'What is it? Elena?'

'No. Not Elena.'

She grabbed her mother's elbow and they wended their way out of the crowd. 'Tell me, please. Your distress is so—'

Her mother's eyes were teary. She grabbed Grace's hand and squeezed. 'It's Declan. There's been an accident. I'm afraid there's not much that can be done.'

'But I just said goodbye to him, not more than four hours ago. The bike?'

'Yes. Not his fault, apparently. A truck's brakes failed. He was swiped from the bike.'

'I must go to him. Mother. I know it's hard. Can you transport me?'

Her mother's hands were shaking. She cupped Grace's face. 'It's risky. I may need to tap into your power. But we can't do it here. There are some exhibition spaces where the old rail-works used to be. We can find a place to hide.'

'Do you know where he is? Can you find it?'

'John Hunter Hospital in Newcastle.'

'Newcastle. He got a long way before…'

They had cleared the station and were passing a series of terraced town houses. Ahead were the old carriage sheds where maintenance used to be carried out on trains. Now they were exhibition and conference spaces. 'Mother, can you take me that far?'

Her mother shook her head. 'No, I can't teleport you with me. But with the help of the council I can send you.'

Grace's head jerked. 'You can send me. Are you sure?'

'It's risky, but there is nothing else to be done for it. Time is short. His parents can't leave yet, but will once Delores can travel. They asked for you. No, they begged for your help.'

'They did?' They took a few more hurried steps and Grace grabbed her mother's hands. 'They understand, don't they, that I can't…you know…bring him back.'

'Yes.'

'Then why did they ask for me?'

Elvira grimaced. 'They want you to do what you can.'

'But what if I can't?'

'Be quiet now. All the councillors have linked with me.'

They found their way into a small storeroom. It was empty and Grace silenced the alarm.

'What should I do?' Tears leaked down her cheeks. Declan was going to die and she didn't know what she could do about it.

'Keep quiet. Stand still.' Elvira leaned forward and planted a kiss on her forehead and then wiped Grace's tears off. 'This will feel strange.'

The air in Grace's lungs froze. She dared not draw breath. Her skin burned like pins and needles, amplified a thousand times. Her mind screamed. The world melted around her but she had to keep very still. It seemed to take forever and then the world solidified. Her breath surged out. Her skin tingled. She was in a different place. She stood outside a large building with doors that swung open as if inviting her in. Through the doors she found people mingling, people in wheelchairs with IVs attached, or people wearing bandages. Walking further in, she found the reception desk. 'May I help you?' said a woman in a dull uniform and glasses on the end of her nose.

'Yes, I'm looking for Declan Mallory. A bike accident. Can you tell me where to find him?'

She checked the screen. 'Are you a relative?'

'I'm his wife. I've just arrived. I got here as soon as I could.'

The receptionist nodded. 'He's in intensive care.' She pulled out a little map. 'Follow these arrows.'

'Thank you.' Grace took the little map and followed the directions. With her witch sense she was seeking out Declan. Her mind touched two other folk in the building. One was a doctor and another a nurse. Folk who served humans. How odd. Grace chewed her lip as she took the lift to intensive care. She couldn't detect Declan at all. *Goddess, let him be alive,* she prayed. *Let him not be gone already.*

Worry creased her forehead. The coven had expended a lot of power to send her there but there was a limit to what she could do. She wanted to be here because she loved Declan. If there were some small thing she could do then she would do it. She sniffed, thinking about his parents asking for her. They must be desperate. Actually, they might recognize her talents.

The intensive care had a front desk. Grace had to wait while the woman behind it talked on the phone and typed information into her computer.

'May I help?' she asked. Grace ceased jumping from foot to foot.

After Grace explained why she was there, the nurse took down her particulars. Lucky, she knew Declan's home address and the name of his parents. When the woman was satisfied she buzzed through to the ward.

'Go through that door. A nurse will meet you and take you through to him.'

Grace thanked her and the other woman gave a tentative smile, one that said, *It's bad. He's going to die.* Grace argued with herself as she walked up the glossy beige hallway. Declan had a room of his own, she saw, as she walked through.

He lay on a bed, a monitor beeping above his head, wires snaking out of him into other monitors and a tube down his throat to help him breathe. Her heart leaped into her throat and she had to fight back tears. 'Declan?'

The nurse checked the monitors and wrote on his chart, while Grace drew close to the bed.

There was nothing from him. No sense of his

presence. A doctor walked in, greeted her and then went to check the monitors. 'You are his wife?' he asked.

'Yes. How bad is it?'

'As bad as it can be.' He checked Declan's eyes with a small torch. 'But we haven't given up yet.'

Grace gently caressed one of Declan's fingers. Half his face was bruised and scraped. His leg had a tent over it. 'What is the damage?'

'Concussion, contusions. We had to operate on his leg but we think it will be all right.'

The nurse asked if she could take a break and after a nod from the doctor, left the room.

The doctor pulled back the sheet to further examine Declan's body. His ribs were stippled with purple and red. Grace sucked in a breath, her fingers brushing against Declan's brow. She closed her eyes and sent her talent into him, seeking something to cling onto.

Declan? Declan!

There was nothing. If she were going to find him, she'd have to go deeper. According to the machines, he was alive.

On opening her eyes, she found the doctor staring at her. 'You're one of the folk, aren't you?' he said in a soft voice.

She swung around. They were alone. The nurse was gone.

Grace gathered her wits and reached out. This was one of the folk she'd sensed earlier. 'Yes. You're from the northern coven?'

He shook his head. 'No coven. A loner. I prefer human ways.'

Grace lifted her chin, indicating Declan. 'Will the human way save him?'

The doctor studied Declan's face. 'I don't know. I

didn't know he was one of the folk as his life energy is so low. Are you really his wife?'

Grace lifted her mouth in a half-smile. 'That's such a loaded question. I love him with all my heart. I'd be his mate if he'd have me. Just this morning he gave me a sweet unproposal. We've been friends since childhood.'

'I understand you have a bond. My name is Lyle Wentz, by the way.'

'Nice to meet you. I'm Grace, from the Sydney coven.'

'So what are you going to do?' he asked. 'The nurse is on a break so we have a short time.'

'That's the problem. I don't know. The coven sent me, but the one talent I have I can't use.'

'What's that?'

'I'm a necromancer.'

Lyle's head jerked up. 'They don't come up often.'

'Tell me about it.'

She stroked Declan's forehead once more, leaning down to brush her lips against the unbruised portion.

'You may not be able to bring him back from the dead, but…well…could you hold him in life until he is over the crisis?'

'What's the crisis?'

'Brain swelling. There's a bleed in there and it's stopped already but the brain swells and that's what's dangerous. It could stop his breathing.'

'Won't that damage his brain too? The swelling, I mean.'

'Yes, there is a possibility, but with human medicine and your magic, we could help him, minimize the damage.'

'Could?'

'He may not want to live.'

Grace concentrated on Declan's face and thought

of their words that morning. He may have been confused about what he wanted to do with his life, but
there was a sense of purpose in him and a joy for life.
There was no way Declan wanted to walk away. 'No,
I can't believe that. What about his spine?'

'Not injured, which in itself is a miracle. Now that
I know he's one of the folk, I'm guessing his talent
must have protected him. The truck driver died in
the accident. Declan's bike was flattened, yet he's rel-
atively intact. His leg will heal in time. Actually, fast,
with folk healing. With determination he'll be back
on his bike again, pretty soon.'

'Okay. I can hold him here. Can you manage the
staff?'

'I'll make sure they let you keep vigil. Just don't
doing anything too flamboyant.'

Grace nodded.

Lyle left her alone. The machines beeped rhyth-
mically. Grace let herself be lulled by the sound. It
helped her sync with Declan. The nurse came back
in, but said nothing. She sat on a stool and tended
tubes and turned Declan as best she could, given his
injuries.

Grace inserted her witch sense into his mind. It
was an empty landscape. No trace of his golden,
glowing presence. She'd have to go deeper, taking
care not to cross over to the other side. That could be
dangerous for her and if Declan had passed over, she
wasn't permitted to bring him back.

Lower down into his consciousness she found a
thin web of his golden essence. Faint but there. She
had to urge him back. Her essence spread out in thin
tendrils, seeking to touch parts of Declan's web.
Nothing happened. Grace chewed her bottom lip.
What could she do? He was alive but sinking fast, as
if he were leaking away. Desperate and in untried

waters, she drew on her own strength and sent it through the fine filaments she had seeking Declan.

Declan. It's me, Grace. Don't leave me. Please.

No response. She fed more of herself into Declan. Let her love for him swell inside her. Her light began to glow around her sense of self. Digging deep into her own reserves meant there was no power for her to screen her emotions from Declan. This was a deep share, deeper than any other. Her love for him came spilling out. Her laughter and joy at being with him. Memories of making love with him tumbled over themselves. *I'd give my life for you, Declan Mallory.*

Grace was on dangerous ground now. She'd fed so much of herself into Declan that she'd lost her sense of self. She had to back away slowly, take herself out of Declan or he could take her with him.

Please, Declan. Fight. Live. Love.

A flicker of something tickled her mind. The threads of Declan's essence were brighter, growing thicker. He was still there. No longer leaving, his essence began to brighten. The thin thread Grace had maintained to her own body thickened.

A breath drew into her lungs and then she exhaled. She was in touch with herself once more. Declan continued to grow stronger. He was not conscious as far as she could tell but he was not on the verge of death. The doctor said she needed to be with him through the crisis. She hoped Lyle would tell her when that would be. Grace's arms and legs were as lead. Her mind was fatigued. She had to shake herself to keep her mind focused and she hung on with dogged determination. There was no sense of time. She was aware of the nurse working around her, of her tending to Declan. The noise of the machines intruded once again. Declan's essence was about half its usual strength, but it was there. He was there.

'Grace?' It was the doctor's voice. 'He's over the worst now. You can relax.'

She heard him. Drawing in a breath, she shuddered once and slid out of Declan's mind. The doctor held up a coffee. 'Here you go. It's been twelve hours.'

Grace couldn't hold the coffee, her hands shook so hard. The doctor tipped it up to her mouth for her. The nurse gave them a strange look. Grace took a few more sips.

The door swung open. Delores and Rohan Mallory walked in. Grace stood up.

'Is he?'

'He's alive,' Grace said, before the world turned sideways. The doctor grabbed her before she fell, spilling the coffee all over them. Lucky it wasn't hot. Grace didn't take in much of anything else in. She fainted.

A few hours later, she woke up in a darkened room, lying on a gurney. She didn't get up. Couldn't get up. Her legs were numb trunks and her arms uncoordinated floppy appendages that refused to obey her commands. Had she been drugged?

Lyle came in with a tray. 'No, you're not drugged. You're drained. When I suggested you hold him here during the crisis, I didn't mean for you to pump all your life force into him.'

'Is that what I did?'

He nodded as he put the tray down. 'Yes. Can you sit up some more?' He adjusted the pillows. 'This is where I nap during breaks in long shifts. It's not the Ritz Carlton, but it's better than the floor.'

'Can you hold this coffee?'

Grace did her best and then shook her head. Lyle tilted the cup so she could sip it. 'How is he?'

'Better. The brain swelling is going down. Another week, he should be over it and ready to go to the ward. Although home is more likely. His parents don't like the hospital. They want to care for him themselves or have their own healer do it.'

Grace took another sip. 'Is that food?'

'A banana. You up for this?' He held it up.

Grace nodded. 'Yes, please.'

He peeled it for her and held it out. She bit down, chewed and then swallowed. The food and coffee were having a marked improvement. Her head had stopped spinning.

'Your mother is here. She has come to take you home by car. When I'm satisfied you are restored enough for the trip I'll wheel you down.'

'Don't you have other patients?'

'Yes, of course I do. But I'm off-duty now.'

'Oh.' Grace ran her fingers through her hair; she must look a fright. Lyle had dark green eyes and they were at that moment studying her. 'Is there something wrong?' she asked.

He shook his blond head. 'No, just thinking that Declan is a lucky man, lucky warlock, I should say. You're a special witch, Grace Riordon.'

Her mouth dropped open. 'How did you know my full name?'

He leaned his back against the wall and smirked. 'Your mother told me, and where to find you if I'm so inclined. No more banana?' He wiggled it back and forth.

'No, I'm done. Mother didn't invite you for dinner, did she? Mention a single witch at our house?'

Lyle chuckled. 'Come to think of it, she did. But I had to tell her I'm married with two kids.'

Grace laughed. 'I bet that pulled her up short.'

He nodded absently, as if remembering the scene.

'I believe it did. Now wait there, I'm wheeling you downstairs.'

A few minutes later he returned with a wheelchair. 'I really don't need this.' She paused, feeling better, but her limbs were not very responsive. 'Okay, maybe I do.'

'Humor me.' He assisted her into the wheelchair. 'No more necromancy for a while. Okay?'

'So is your wife human?' she asked as he wheeled her into the corridor.

'Yes. So was my mother.'

They bumped into the lift doors. Lyle wasn't a good driver. 'You don't push wheelchairs much, do you?'

'No, but you'll arrive in one piece, I promise. Now, I want you to go home and rest. You need to eat lots of fresh vegetables and fruit. Wholesome food to restore your life force. Declan is on the mend and out of danger thanks to you. Let me help him now and I'll even mind the parents.'

The lift whooshed open. In a short time, Grace could see Elvira with Robertson, one of the other councillors. Her mother didn't smile, but Grace detected the sweep of her mother's witch sense checking that she was okay. Grace waved to Robertson. He blushed deeply. He was a rather shy warlock, and probably a bit afraid of her mother. Come to think of it, afraid of her too.

'Thank you, young man. You know how to get in touch with me now. I expect updates on Declan's condition.'

Lyle agreed, then with a wink at Grace he sauntered off, soon lost in the throng of people heading to lifts or medical appointments.

'Come on, dear. We'll take you home. Robertson, here, drove. I was too distracted.'

After a nod from Elvira, Robertson grabbed her wheelchair and began to wend his way through people out to the door. He'd parked in the no standing zone. There was a parking inspector issuing tickets, but none were on his car. Grace grinned. Cheeky warlock.

With a last forlorn look at the hospital and her empty wheelchair on the pavement, Grace said a silent goodbye to Declan. She had no idea if he would ever know the part she'd played in his survival.

CHAPTER TEN

After two weeks in bed recuperating and being plied with her mother's concoctions, listening to Elena's descriptions of her latest craft project and Fel's annoying anecdotes, Grace was allowed out of her room. News had reached them of Declan's progress. After Dr Wentz deemed him well enough, his parents had him transferred to the Blue Mountains and into Beatrice the healer's care.

Grace continued her life as usual, except for the empty spot where Declan had been. There were no messages from him and no communication from his parents. It was if he'd ridden off that day and hadn't come back. The trip to the hospital, her joining her essence with his, faded to a distant memory.

On the sofa Grace sat alone, stroking Fel's filmy substance absently as she watched how the light changed outside as the sun went down.

Scratch? Fel stuck its muzzle into her face.

Automatically, Grace obeyed Fel's request, using her fingers to ease Fel's itchy bits. Though how a dead cat could feel it was beyond her understanding.

A glass of red wine appeared in front of her. Startled, she looked up. 'Elena. I didn't know you were home.' She took the glass and shuffled over to make room.

Fel meowed indignantly and sauntered away.

'My class was cancelled.' Elena fetched a glass for herself and then snuggled next to Grace. 'Cheers.' Elena touched her glass to Grace's. 'You're sad. I don't like seeing it.'

Grace tossed back some of the wine. 'Not sad, but low. I'm a little low, energy wise, heart wise, mind wise.'

'Elvira said it will take time to recover. What you did was remarkable. She told me that if she'd been with you, she wouldn't have let you expend so much of yourself to save him.'

'I did what anyone would have done.'

Elena shook her head. 'Not anyone. Elvira said there hasn't been a talent like yours for fifty years at least. She said you saved his mother and then him.'

A smile spread across her face. 'She's my mother. Of course she's going to say nice things about me. It's what mothers do.'

Elena's arm snaked across her shoulders. 'You think that, darling Grace, if it makes you feel better.'

With her wine finished, Grace climbed to her feet and refilled their glasses. A slight dizziness hit. A half glass of wine didn't normal affect her like that. She tipped some more wine into their glasses and then sipped hers slowly. It was a mild evening and the trees were now shadows. Elena played with her hair and talked softly.

While they chatted, Fel begged for a cuddle first from Elena and then Grace, until it ultimately curled up on the arm of the sofa, content to just be, even if it was a ghostly being.

Elvira was out for the evening. 'New man,' Elena

whispered conspiratorially as if her mother would overhear and think it disrespectful.

'Go her. I have my hand vibrator to keep me company.'

Elena laughed so hard she fell off the sofa.

'What? Don't you use one? Mine's called Randy Roger.' Grace looked on while Elena rolled around the floor, laughing so hard she cried.

Grace rolled her eyes up to the ceiling. 'Obviously, you need to do more work to get in touch with your inner rhythms. Sex is natural and now that I know just the thought of one sends you into a fit of giggles, I'm going to buy you one and lend you a book.'

'A book?' The red-faced Elena gasped out.

'Yes, a book from school.'

Elena crawled into a sitting position on the floor and rested her head on the sofa cushion. 'You mean like sex education?'

'That's the one.'

Fatigue was wearing Grace down so she wished Elena good night and staggered down the hall. She took a hot shower, climbed into her pajamas and rolled into bed. Fel wasn't on the bed cover so she assumed the cat had taken up residence with Elena for the night. A light wind ruffled the curtains and weak moonlight bathed the yard. She laid back on the bed, fatigue numbing her limbs and slowly seducing her mind to sleep.

Lips on hers jolted her awake. She sat up in bed and scanned the room. No one was there with her. It had seemed so real. After taking a few deep breaths, she calmed back down again and closed her eyes. Lips were on hers again and her eyes flew open. This time she could taste the magic in the air. Lunging out of the bed, she raced to the window and threw it up. 'Declan?'

Shrubbery ate the sound of her voice. She stood motionless, listening. It couldn't be a dream. That was definitely magic. Could he have sent that kiss all the way from the Blue Mountains? Perhaps. Maybe.

There was no point in going back to bed. Not if she was either dreaming of kisses or being kissed magically. She slipped on a thin robe and stepped outside. Stars flickered faintly overhead, drowned out by the light of the city. The wind had scented the air with salt from the harbor. Leaves rustled and then she turned. A tall silhouette stood there. She closed her eyes and reached out. It was Declan, whole and healthy.

He was there in an instant, his warm body enveloping her, his face buried in her hair. 'Grace.'

Silently she held him, too choked up for words. He released her and she lifted her head to gaze at him, touching his cheek with the back of her finger. It was a sweet face.

'You saved me. I owe you my life.'

Grace shook her head. 'No, you don't.'

'But...'

'Shhh...' She placed her finger on his lips. 'You have your life, Declan. You owe me nothing. You are free to go, if that's what you want.'

'I felt your presence.'

Grace widened her eyes. She'd thought he might have done, but wasn't sure. 'What do you remember?'

'I remember your love for me.'

'Figures.'

He cupped her face. 'I love you, Grace. Leaving you was one of the hardest things I have ever done. I was heading back when...you know. Now after the accident, I came to the conclusion that life is too short to put off what you want to do, what you must do.'

'What are you saying?'

'I want to join with you. Settle down.'

Grace stepped back and rubbed at her upper arms. 'This isn't you talking.'

'No, don't go.' He drew her back into his arms and rested his forehead against hers. 'It is me talking. I would have died if it weren't for you. But it's not gratitude that brings me here. You knew I loved you before I left, but I was so confused and pig-headed that I didn't value you the way I should have.'

'That's true.' Grace smiled to herself. 'Your parents would never agree to you joining with me. There are stacks of other witches dying to be with you.'

'Not as many as you would think?'

Grace's mouth dropped open. 'What do you mean?'

'Apparently there is a rumor circulating that I'm rather under-endowed where it counts.'

'Oh?'

He grabbed her to him so that she draped against him. 'Really, Grace. Under-endowed? Did you have to start that rumor?'

She had a rather healthy impression of his en-dowment at that moment. 'Well, you had to be there.'

'Danila? Figures. I didn't sleep with her. She did take off her clothes, which is where my mother got the idea. I told her to put them back on. I was rather ill-tempered, actually. I may have said she disgusted me, which isn't very gentlemanly but I was provoked.'

'I knew you hadn't slept with her. Or if you had, you'd made a poor impression. No one could have been laid by you and been so unaffected.'

'Grace Riordon, if you don't stop talking like that

I'm going to stretch you out on this bit of lawn and have my way with you.'

Grace kept on talking. She liked the smell of dewy grass. 'I mean, I could hardly walk after—'

Declan had her under him so fast she didn't notice until she saw the stars overhead. 'Is that a battle mage technique? Because it could come in handy to—'

Her words were cut off by Declan's savage kiss. She rather liked his rough and ready approach and responded in kind, tugging his hair as she thoroughly explored his mouth with her tongue.

Wrestling in the grass had advantages. She wasn't likely to fall off anything as they squirmed and writhed together. Declan was growling as he aggressively tugged down her pajama bottoms, gaining access to her.

However, she wasn't taking that lying down, so she raked her nails across his back where she'd been previously enjoying his smooth skin under her fingers. Declan grabbed a handful of her hair and kissed her soundly. They tumbled together with her in a pajama top and he in jeans half down his backside. That wasn't good enough. Grace gripped a butt cheek until he squeaked. 'Take them off,' she demanded.

Too busy with his hands to comply, he magicked them off. Tugging at her pajamas was getting him nowhere. 'Tear them,' she said breathily as she bit his shoulder. The sound of the material ripping tipped her excitement over the edge. Her heart thudded in her belly before leaping to her throat. She had to have him inside of her. There was a space where he was meant to be and if he didn't get to it, she was likely to rip his head off from sheer need.

'Take me now.'

'No.' He paused, cradling her head in his two hands and kissing the tip of her nose.

'No?'

'No.'

She scrunched up her brows and started flicking through possible hexes she could hurl at him. 'What are you doing then?'

He sighed. 'You don't get it. I love you, Grace. I want to be with you. Have a life with you. I'm serious. Take a look if you don't believe me.'

With trembling hands, she traced one eyebrow and then the other. With a soft inhale she slipped inside his mind. He was golden and warm and a thousand times more powerful than when she'd last shared this space with him. His love for her penetrated her deep. Gone were the confusion and the anger. A kernel of love pulsated for her.

Grace revealed herself to him. All the love she had stored away. Their minds were still entwined as he entered her. Their bodies moved together slowly, so caught up in the love they shared, a bridge between their essence and their bodies. When they came together, Grace was tugged deeper into Declan and there she experienced his inner beauty and the power of him. He loved her. He wanted to be with her. His hopes and dreams were there. Silently, she assured him that he could pursue them. She would stand by his side.

Later as the sun rose, they lay together. 'Declan?'

'Yes,' he said as he rolled her toward him and kissed her forehead.

'Will you want children?'

He kissed her nose. 'Yes.'

She snuggled into him and he spoke into her ear softly. 'Do you mind if we hold off for a year or two on having a baby?' he said.

She drew back, watched his mouth has he spoke, not quite believing they were having this discussion when a few hours ago it had seemed impossible. 'I know there's pressure and all that from the coven, but you have things you want to do. I have things I want you to do, with setting up a school for teaching battle mages.'

She cupped his face and stared longingly into his dark eyes.

'Will that make you happy?' he asked.

'Yes.' Her voice was soft, dreamy, sated.

'I take it then that you're agreeing to join with me.'

'Yes,' she said in the same languid way.

'And are you tossing Randy Roger away?'

Her eyes widened. 'Not quite yet.'

He grabbed for her, but she rolled away and ran into the house, putting up a shield so no one would see them running naked. Declan thundered after her.

Grace hailed Elena to let her know it was just Declan. They headed for the shower, where she took great delight in soaping him all over and washing him off. Declan had a bit more trouble accomplishing the same task with her.

He'd started with her breasts and before he'd moved to other parts of her body, he flattened her face-first against the wall and took her that way. Grace loved to have him inside her. The water and the soap washed away, leaving his erection piercing her again and again.

By the time he was done, she was limp. He carried her to bed, dried her off and then rolled under the covers with her. Grace had been ready for sleep until Declan put his mouth on her. It didn't take long before she was screaming his name. Grace cringed at the amount of noise she was making. They'd have to get a special ward for their bedroom when they joined. She hoped her mother wasn't home. It had been embarrassing enough the last time.

Sufficiently alert, Grace attacked Declan's cock with her tongue. It didn't take him long to start shouting her name, equally loudly. They were definitely going to need a special noise-reducing ward.

A satisfied grin on her face disappeared when Declan tossed her back against the mattress and fell on her, dragging her hips and skewering her within seconds. Her breath grew ragged as he pumped into her. She arched her back, meeting him thrust for thrust. Using her witch sense, she touched his mind. A minute touch was enough to send her spiraling into ecstasy herself. Declan was in the moment. It was grind and grind and rippling electricity, from his cock to his gut. Grace's sex throbbed as her climax broke over her. Utterly shattered, she lay in Declan's arms until her stomach rumbled.

'You're hungry. I'll get you something.'

'No. It's all right. I hailed Elena. She'll bring us something.'

Declan nuzzled with his nose below her ear. 'Smart witch.'

It was moments like these where one put up with one's cousin's cooking. The smell of coffee and burnt toast reached them a short while later. 'Maybe I'm not so smart.'

Declan dragged the tray in that Elena had left outside her door. She sent her cousin thanks and scraped the charcoal off her toast and layered it in jam.

They were drinking their second coffee when they sensed the others arrive.

'My mother.'

'My parents.'

Grace cringed. 'I think your clothes are on the front lawn.'

Declan dived out of bed and went to the window. Their clothes flew into his hands. 'Not anymore.'

Grace climbed out of bed and winced as she stood. They had been rather vigorous. 'I suppose we have to face them.'

Grace dreaded meeting Declan's parents again. Could she have a relationship where the parents of her partner hated her so much? Family was everything to her. It was her life, her centre. Elvira could and did care for Declan. Elena and he had been close since Elena had come to live with them. Could she live within the centre of two circles, where she wasn't loved? She loved Declan with her whole self.

A lot could be sacrificed for that love. But in her heart she knew that unkindness, hatred and being shunned would wear her down, would impact negatively on them. What of any children? Could she really bring them into a family that was riddled with such negativity? Right then, she needed the wise words of her mother. Although the decision would be hers, she valued her mother's council.

Grace slipped on some jeans and then limped around the room, looking for some shoes. Declan sat on the bed and watched her, a lopsided grin on his face.

'What's so funny? Meeting your folks is not a joke.'

'I know that. But seeing you limp will certainly dispel the rumors about my...' He waggled his little finger. 'My mother was quite shocked when she heard that story.'

Grace bit her lip. 'You're funning me. She couldn't have heard that.'

He leaned over and tapped her on the bottom.

'I'm not funning you. Lighten up. You might be surprised.'

He stood up and bowed and then held out his elbow. 'Come on. Let me assist you from the room. I believe your mother has summoned us.'

Grace's stomach was doing flip-flops. Her life would be affected by the next ten minutes. She would either be certain of where she was going forward or suddenly bereft. Declan would stand by her, but she couldn't bear to be the cause of a major rift.

Her mother stood, moving from foot to foot. On the sofa, Rohan and Delores Mallory sat. When their eyes fell on Declan, they visibly relaxed.

'So good of you to join us. I believe it's time we all had a little chat, don't you?' her mother said, with a layer of smugness in her voice.

Declan fetched up two dining chairs and brought them over. He grinned at his parents and then grinned at Grace.

Grace sat down, straightened her top, and fiddled with her socks. She moved over slightly to make room for Declan. 'So, what is it we need to discuss?' Declan asked.

Delores sat forward and quickly dropped her gaze to her knee where she played with the hem of her skirt. 'Son…is this the witch you have chosen to join with?'

'Yes, I've chosen Grace.'

'Are you sure about this?' his father asked. 'You were confused before. You told me you didn't want to settle down.'

'That's true. I didn't want to settle down just yet. But it's always been Grace for me. I told her before I left that that if I was to settle it would be with her. Now, after a near-death experience, there is no point putting off what you want to do. You need to do it and as many of the things you want to do while you can. I didn't think I could have Grace and the things I wanted. Now I know I will make it work.' He glanced and her and took her hand. 'We will make it work.'

Elvira sat down in a chair and hitched it forward. 'You see, I told you. What is to be done?'

'Done? Why does anything have to be done?' Grace asked.

'Well, you can't stay here accommodating this under-endowed warlock rather noisily.'

Grace sucked in a breath as her face radiated heat like a beacon. 'Mother? Who told you about that?' To Declan's parents she said, 'I'm so sorry. I don't normally say such things…'

'She was provoked,' added Declan with a wide grin.

'Elena told me.' Elvira snuck in.

'She's such a blabbermouth.'

Rohan and Delores looked from one to the other, a question on their lips.

Declan took pity on them. 'Danila.'

Delores nodded, but appeared none the wiser. 'My son is not under-endowed. Well, he wasn't last time I looked.' Her husband jabbed her in the ribs with his elbow.

'They can have our house. We will move to the house at Leura,' Rohan Mallory said.

Delores sought Grace's gaze. 'That is, if it is all right with you?'

Grace opened and shut her mouth and jerked her head at Declan. Picking up her cue, he thanked his parents. 'I haven't had a chance to talk to Grace, but I'm sure that would be great. She's too overcome to speak.'

Grace was overcome. She was expecting recriminations, yelling, screaming and perhaps hair pulling. She waggled her eyebrows at her mother.

Elvira inclined her head, a slight smile evident. 'That is very generous of you. I will assist them with their own furniture. We will need to consult with the council about a joining ceremony.

'By the way, Grace darling, in light of your services to the coven, you have been offered work for the council. Real work.'

Grace shared an incredulous look with Declan. He appeared to be taking it in his stride. He must have known. This must be the thing he said she needed time to do. Looking around the room, to her mother and his parents, she was amazed. She'd never in her dreams expected this moment would come. They were discussing her joining with Declan calmly. He leaned over and kissed her cheek. Grace wanted to say over and over again that she didn't understand. It was meant to be difficult. As she listened to their parents discussing their union, she let go of the tension, the ropes strapping her heart up tight.

It was then the tears started. She wiped at them and sniffed. She didn't mean to cry. Declan lifted her hand and kissed her knuckle. 'You knew,' she accused, sniffing loudly.

He tilted his head and grinned. 'I had an inkling.'

'Grace?' her mother said.

Grace shook her head, not quite able to speak.

She didn't want to mind speak to her mother either, because the others would know and that would be rude. This was an uneasy alliance at best. She didn't want to offend them.

'Mother, please thank the council, but I think I want to spend some time with Declan first and then I'll talk to them about a job. You know, get to know each other. But in a few months, I'll be ready.'

Delores stood up suddenly. 'Please, will you all give me a moment alone with Grace?'

Declan's eyebrows twitched and then he stood up. His father led the way. Elvira was not as keen to leave until she got a nod from Grace.

Delores took a few steps around the room. She scrunched her dress in her hands. 'Forgive me. I don't know where to begin. There's so much…' She sat back down again. 'I must thank you for what you did for me. I was a tormented person. I didn't know what I had been carrying all those years.' She made eye contact with Grace. 'It is so easy to hate, easy to let it fester. You were always so full of joy, even when you were young…especially when you were young. I was envious of you even then, of Declan's love for you. Nothing seemed to separate you.'

She reached out a hand. Grace took it, although she was reluctant. On contact she could tell that Delores spoke the truth from the heart. 'I can see with clear eyes now and a clear heart. I ask you to forgive me for how I treated you.'

'I do forgive you.'

'I have another important favor to ask.'

Grace nodded, dreading that it would be a plea to walk away and leave Declan. She held her breath, getting nothing from Delores through the skin contact. She was shielding herself.

'Accept us into your life. Please, I beg you. I know

you have no reason to and we won't interfere much; we are going to the mountains. But we do so much want to be part of Declan's life.'

Grace went down her on knees and looked up into Delores's eyes. 'That is what I want more than anything. Family is important to me. What you have said has made me feel so happy. I don't want to exclude you. Declan loves you and I couldn't do anything to make him unhappy. Forget about the past, Delores. I have. There is nothing there now but my love for Declan.'

Delores touched her hair and sniffed. "I have more to say. From my heart I want to thank for my son's life. I know you gave of your own life force to keep him in this world. That nice Dr Wentz told me. Your mother made the council join together to send you. Do you know how remarkable that is? The council hardly ever work together."

Grace sat next to Delores and hugged her. The woman sobbed and Grace rocked her back and forth. She was free of that taint, the fragment of her dead brother. Yet, there was an ingrained sadness in her, one that Grace vowed not to increase.

'Can I get you something?'

Delores looked up and blinked at the tissue Grace extended. 'Dinner?'

Grace frowned. 'I don't understand.'

'Your mother said you would cook for us.'

Grace lifted her chin. 'My mother is a sly witch. Excuse me while I tell them to come in. Mother has an appointment with some potatoes.'

Sometime later, after a big meal of roast lamb and all the trimmings, Grace lay back against Declan on the sofa with her eyes clothed.

'Are you happy?' Declan asked, kissing the top of her ear.

'More than I thought possible. I love you more than anything, but it would have been so hard to be with you if your parents hated me.'

The hand that was caressing her stilled. 'So if my parents detested you, then you wouldn't be with me?'

Grace turned around and bumped heads with him. 'It would have taken some convincing.'

'Right then.' Grace leapt off the sofa and screamed as she was chased into her room. Declan caught her in the hall. 'Your mother is out, isn't she?'

A door opened. 'But I'm in,' said Elena. There was a meow from around her feet.

So am I. Tell your big tom to keep it down.

He is a big tom, isn't he? Grace thought to the cat. I don't think he can keep it down.

Grace burst out laughing. Elena picked up the cat. 'You talking to the cat again, Grace?'

That made Grace laugh harder.

'Good night, Elena. Use earplugs,' Declan said as he scooped up Grace and kicked open the door.

Grace squeaked and then all the air exploded out of her as she landed on the bed, closely followed by a very large man.

Now, where were we?

You were going to convince me.

His lips captured her hungry mouth. Touching heads, touching minds. Grace let herself sink into the warm golden glow that was her man. His energy pervaded her, giving back the last vestiges of the power she'd given him. Her body was energized. The fingers that peeled off her top left ripples of electricity in their wake.

How am I doing so far?

Fair to middling.

He slapped her bottom. 'I love you, Grace Riordon. I'm looking forward to spending my life with you.'

He kissed down the column of her throat, then across to her breasts. Grace cried out when he latched onto her nipple. She grabbed a handful of his hair and pulled. He grinned at her and lunged for the other breast.

'Declan Mallory, consider yourself joined.' She pushed at his shoulders and he obligingly flopped over onto his back. His expression grew serious as he traced a finger along her chin.

'What is it?' she asked.

'I love the joy in you. It's infectious.'

Grace chewed her lip. 'That's nice, but what is really bothering you? Don't make me go in there and fish it out.'

'I'd like to see you try that. I've been working on my shielding. You may only get past my guard if I'm unconscious and I trust'—He poked her softly on the nose—'that you will be honorable.'

'I always am honorable.' She looked from side to side. 'Well, mostly...' She would never stop being embarrassed about the under-endowed rumor. 'And that's not it. Spill.'

'Are you really okay with holding off on having children?' His voice was hushed.

'Of course I'm okay with it. I want a couple of years to work over your body and then maybe, just maybe, I'll think of sharing you with a child.'

Declan gaped at her for a moment and then dissolved in a fit of laughter.

'What did I say?'

'You work over my body? A little thing like you?'

Her grin was very wide. 'Yes, a little thing like me. Now, if you would just cooperate by taking off your clothes, I think we should start, unless I have to bring out Randy Roger.'

Her man erupted off the bed and had her flat on her back and naked in thirty seconds. 'I'm afraid your predilection for small, underendowed appliances will have to end.'

'You think so?'

He ground his heavy erection and against her. 'I know so.'

Grace sighed with pure pleasure as Declan very slowly, very gently made love to her, with his mind and with his body.

I love you, Declan Mallory.

And I love you, Grace Riordon.

AFTERWORD

Thanks for reading *Spiritbound*. I hope you enjoyed it.

If you'd like to know more about me, my books, or to connect with me online, you can visit my webpage danikristoff.wordpress.com, follow me on twitter @dani_kristoff, or like my Facebook page facebook.com/danikristoff

Reviews can help readers find books, and I am grateful for all honest reviews. Thank you for taking the time to let others know what you've read, and what you thought.

You've just read a book in the *Spellbound* series. The next book in this series is *Bespelled*.

ACKNOWLEDGEMENTS 2016

It's wonderful to have first readers to help you shape a book. For *Spiritbound*, I have to thank Nicole Murphy, who told me I had to write Grace and Declan's story in the first place and who also gave me feedback on the first draft. A big thank you to Cora Wright, who gave fantastic feedback too. I have to confess to Cora that I still think there are some rainbows left in the story. The lovely Joanne Anderton and Ingrid Jonach gave some insightful tips as well.

Spiritbound wouldn't have been written without the encouragement of Kate Cuthbert, who provided so much guidance when I wrote *Bespelled*, my first paranormal romance. This story benefitted from the lessons she taught me. I believe they are forever engraved on my brain.

I'd also like to thank Harlequin and the Escape Publishing team for all the hard work they have done to make the imprint a success and I'm so proud and happy to be working with such a great collection of writers. I certainly never want for reading material.

ACKNOWLEDGMENTS 2019

Spiritbound has a new lease on life. Even though I think Grace and Declan's story is special, the highlight of the novel though, for me, is the relationship Grace has with her mother and cousin. It's also about the positive feels the story has, even when discussing some dark themes.

I hope you enjoy this book as much as I did writing it. I'd like to thank Nicole Murphy and Keri Arthur for cover advice on this version and for general support in my paranormal romance writing adventures.

I'd like to thank those who nominated this book for the Australian Romance Readers Award in 2016. That was a special moment. Thank you so much.

Donna
November 2019

ABOUT THE AUTHOR

Dani Kristoff is a Canberra-based author, who delights in reading and writing paranormal romance. She's been writing since late 2000, which means nearly twenty years, although she's been concentrating her efforts on science fiction, fantasy and horror. Published both traditionally and independently, she's currently undertaking a PhD in creative writing at the University of Canberra. Her research area is feminism and romance. Her partner is also a writer and they get up to geekery whenever possible.

www.ingramcontent.com/pod-product-compliance
Lightning Source LLC
Chambersburg PA
CBHW050848190726
48286CB00007B/2284